"Are you Paisley Ter

"Bobby Trumane would like you to meet him at the airport."

My brows twitched up in disbelief. I wasn't going anywhere with Bobby, of all people.

"I thought you'd say that."

I leaned in toward the limo and almost died when Bobby stepped out. He looked so damn good, it was unbelievable, like he had just stepped off the pages of *GQ* magazine. It had been only a few months, but this was not the same man I had busted on national TV.

"Let's talk," he said before I could even say hello.

"About what?" I crossed my arms. "And how did you find me?"

"I wanted to surprise you with a trip. You won't have to spend a dime."

"Where did you get the money for all of this?" I motioned toward the limo.

"I know you always thought I was dreaming big, baby. But I signed not one but two NBA clients."

Damn, I thought. *Why couldn't he have hit a lick like that when we were together?*

"Come on, Paisley." Bobby stepped closer to me. "You stood by me when I was flat broke. Let me repay you." A huge smile crossed his face.

I couldn't believe I was standing outside my boyfriend's condo contemplating whether I should take a free weekend getaway with my ex.

MEN, MONEY, & GOLD DIGGERS

Je'Caryous Johnson

GRAND CENTRAL PUBLISHING

NEW YORK BOSTON

This book is a work of fiction. Names, characters, places, and incidents are the product of the author's imagination or are used fictitiously. Any resemblance to actual events, locales, or persons, living or dead, is coincidental.

Grand Central Publishing
Hachette Book Group
237 Park Avenue
New York, NY 10017

Visit our Web site at www.HachetteBookGroup.com.

Printed in the United States of America

First Edition: February 2009
10 9 8 7 6 5 4 3 2 1

Grand Central Publishing is a division of Hachette Book Group, Inc.
The Grand Central Publishing name and logo is a trademark of Hachette Book Group, Inc.

Library of Congress Cataloging-in-Publication Data

Johnson, Je'Caryous.
Men, money, & gold diggers / Je'Caryous Johnson. — 1st ed.
p. cm.
Summary: "Can a man with money ever find true love? That's the question that Caleb Peterson continually asks himself in this novel"—Provided by the publisher.
ISBN 978-0-446-54108-4
1. African Americans—Fiction. 2. Rich people—Fiction. 3. Male selection—Fiction. I. Title.
PS3610.O3555M46 2009
813'.6—dc22
2008033188

Book design and text composition by L&G McRee

Dedication

Standing on the front porch, hearing the birds chirp and watching a beautiful breeze sweep across everyone's brow, I see her. My grandmother . . . the strangest smile dancing across her face.

I ask, "Are you ready for your walk?"

"I guess so," she replies. "I need to get some exercise in this old body. Seems like it just doesn't want to act right."

Immediately I go to her and grab her hand, a hand that has seventy-two years' worth of strength in it.

"I hope we are not going to walk too far. I can't go as long as I used to or walk as far as you," she says.

"Don't worry, we'll just make the block," I tell her.

Down the street we walk, around the corner on the same paved road that I played on as a child. I couldn't help but reminisce about the many times this wonderful woman stood on the porch where we now began our daily walks and yelled out my name when the streetlights came on. A sign that playtime was over.

Now here we are . . . standing in the parking lot of a high school that four generations of my family attended. She looks at it, taking it all in, then dispenses some uncanny wisdom: "The world doesn't slow down, you know; only people."

We sit on a bench, and I lean over to her and kiss her on her cheek, saying, "I love you, Grandma."

"I love you too, honey," she replies.

Another few minutes go by as we just sit and relax. A pigeon walks up to us and sits on the other end of the bench, next to Grandma. And it's just the three of us. She, me, and a bird—an oddly strange yet remarkably beautiful bird that has the freedom to fly to places we can only imagine. The bird jumps into her lap, startling me, but Grandma sits there with the strength of a marble statue. I watch in awe as this bird lays its head on her, as if it too was longing for a piece of her wisdom. We get a great laugh out of it.

"You ready?" I finally ask.

"Yeah," she smiles. "I'm ready to go home."

We stand up, and the courageous bird flies away, toward the direction of home, as if it were some kind of guide. We follow. When we get to the house, I stop, but Grandma keeps going. She goes farther than I ever could, to places where the courageous birds go.

You go, Grandma; you fly away . . . lift your wings and soar through Heaven. I'm walking for you down here, strutting your stroll and continuing your legacy. We are okay. You just fly on, Grandma, side by side with God. Save a spot for me, though, for one day, we will all sit together again.

This book is dedicated to you,
Lois Loretta Young Guidry Johnson, my grandma.

Acknowledgments

I must first give honor to You, God, and thank You for Your presence and Your promise to Your people so that we may fulfill Your purpose. It is in Your will and name that I complete my first novel. Without You, none of this would be possible. You are truly a wonderful and awesome God. I thank You for all that You have done in my life.

Where do I begin? To my mom, Manon C. Johnson, who had me at sixteen years old. Although you put your dreams aside to take care of me, you never stopped encouraging my dreams. No matter how crazy my ideas were, you never said they weren't going to work (even when they didn't). I can never repay you for all the love, time, and energy you put into me, but I will do my best to come close.

To the best sisters in the whole world—Miracah, Simone, and Angela—the three angels in my corner. When everyone else doubted me, I could always count on you to stand by me. We've come a long way, but it ain't over yet!

Thanks also to Francis and Little Frank. I look up to you just as much as you look up to me.

Grandma and Grandpa, my heroes, my spiritual role models, you are the epitome of strength. I will always love and admire you both. Although you're not here in the flesh, I know you are here in the spirit. As you look down on me from Heaven, I pray I make you proud.

To my father, Frank Z. McClain, thank you for being a friend when I needed you to be one. No matter what, I know with you in my corner I'll always have at least one fan.

Eugene McDaniel, the man who taught me all I know about writing, thank you for the pep talks and pushing me to be the best I can be.

Gary Guidry, my uncle, business partner, and friend, thank you for seeing the vision and helping me to grow it to fruition. We have gone through the trenches and back again. Let's keep on Keeping on. Also, lots of love to Mona, Taylor, and Paige.

To the I'm Ready Productions Inc. family, ReShonda, Carla, Jai, Javon, Jeremy, Pat, and Mandell. You are the most talented group of people I know. I could not do this without you guys.

My fans who have faithfully come to see all of my plays with I'm Ready Productions Inc., you have supported me over and over and over again as I poured out my soul to you. Thank you for lifting me up. I promise I won't let you down.

To the Johnson family, it is said that it takes a whole village to raise a child. Thank you for being the village behind me. You guys gave me your last dime so that one of us in the family could make it. I'm glad it was me.

To my two best friends: Ashley Pryor and Jovan Means—what is success without someone you love to share it with?

To Dennis and Prize and Dr. Durrett, thank you for always having my back.

To my spiritual leaders, Pastor Terrence Johnson of Higher

Dimension and Bishop James Dixon of the Community of Faith, thank you for teaching me to have faith in my work, for work without faith is void.

To my agents, Charles King and Jay Mandel, and my lawyers, Erach, Wendle, Nina, and Brian, thank you for being my dream team.

To my publicist Lisa Sorenson, thank you for believing I have a voice that's worthy to be heard.

Ha–G and Debbie May, the two best tour managers in the world. Thank you for holding my tours together and keeping me from falling apart.

To Richard Greer, the most humble and benevolent person I know. Many of our tours would not have happened if it wasn't for you. You're the best.

And to all the people that I didn't mention, know that it doesn't diminish your place in my life. They just told me I couldn't thank everybody. Catch you in the next book.

To Sharony, Angela, and all the talented crew at *Essence* magazine, thank you for listening.

To all of the wonderful actors I have had the pleasure of working with, you know who you are. Thank you for allowing me to be a part of your lives. I will never forget the wonderful memories you gave me.

To my newfound book family, Karen Thomas and Linda Duggins. This is the first of many.

I hope you like it, and I look forward to the future. Hit me up at jjohnson@imreadyproductions.com or www.JeCaryousJohnson.com. And make sure you check out the I'm Ready Web site at www.imreadyproductions.com.

Until next time,
Keep praying, keep loving, keep living, keep playing. . . .

MEN, MONEY, & GOLD DIGGERS

Prologue

Caleb

This heifer has lost her mind.

My grandmother would turn over in her grave if she heard me talking about a woman like that, but there simply was no other way to describe the woman standing in the middle of the living room, all puffy-eyed, honey blonde curls cascading down her back, wearing a see-through, four-hundred-dollar Dolce & Gabbana nightgown that my dumb behind was stupid enough to buy.

"Caleb, let me explain," she cried.

I looked at her, back at him. "So this can be explained?" I glared at her as if she were crazy. How the hell could she explain this?

"Look, man, my beef ain't with you," he said.

I stared at him, taking in all six feet two inches of him, wondering if I hauled off and knocked him in his chiseled jaw right now, would he think showing up here had been a bad idea.

"Let me get this straight," I said, trying my best to stay calm. "You show up at *my* girl's crib in the middle of the night, pissed off at *my* girl 'cause she's here with *me*?"

I paced back and forth, trying to remember the speech my grandmother used to always give me about controlling my anger. *Count to ten, baby*. I heard her voice in my head as if she were right there in the room with me.

I counted to twenty. It wasn't working.

Kendra walked over and tried to rub my arm. I instinctively jerked away. "Baby, please. It's not like it seems," she said.

"Son, are you okay?"

I turned toward my father. I had forgotten he was even in the room. The commotion had brought him out of the guest room. Out of all the nights for this stuff to go down, it had to happen while my dad was visiting from Atlanta.

"Naw, Pops, I'm straight," I said. "I got this."

"Dad, I'm so sorry you had to witness this. It's been over for a while with me and Tony," Kendra said, tears filling her eyes.

"Dad?" Tony snapped. "I know you didn't! Two weeks ago, you were all up in *my* parents' face, talking about Mama and Daddy."

I swear, I didn't think a black woman's face could turn white, but all the color seemed to instantly drain from Kendra's caramel-colored face.

"Tony, why are you doing this?" she whined.

"What did you think?" he yelled. "You got this dude lying up in a bed my money bought, and I'm supposed to be okay with that?"

"Hold on." I looked back and forth between Kendra and Tony. At one time, I thought she was supermodel beautiful, with her exotic looks and perfect figure. But right about now, she was one of the ugliest women I'd ever seen. "I'm confused," I continued, trying to process everything. Kendra and I have been together for six months and she'd just moved into this condo a month ago. She hadn't bought anything new, with the exception of her king-size sleigh bed and bedroom set, which she'd just bought with her tax refund check. Or so she said.

I turned to Kendra as reality set in. "Tell me he did not buy this bed."

She lowered her head in shame.

"I bought the whole bedroom set!" Tony yelled.

At that point, I couldn't help but laugh. I know they thought I was crazy, but I guess at that moment, I had to laugh to keep from crying. Kendra was a piece of work. I couldn't believe I was caught up in some madness like this. In addition to making well over six figures, I wasn't lacking in the looks department. People are always telling me I look like a slightly darker version of the actor Shemar Moore, with a swagger like Denzel Washington, so I never had a problem getting women. It just seemed that I kept getting the wrong women.

"Why are you laughing, Caleb?" she said, obviously not knowing what to make of my sudden outburst of laughter.

"Dang, girl, you good." I turned to Tony. "You bought the bedroom set, huh?"

He nodded.

"Well, ain't that something. I bought the living room and dining room set." I shook my head, still not believing this. Kendra and I hadn't been together real long, but we definitely were serious about each other. Or so I thought.

Tony, the bonehead standing in my living room right now, was supposed to be a thing of the past. *Supposed* to be.

"Caleb, please. I'm begging you, let me explain." She reached out to try to grab my arm. I had to reach back and catch myself because I was about to knock the mess outta her.

"It's over between me and Tony," she cried. "I don't want him. I want *you*."

Tony walked over and grabbed her. "Why are you doing this?" he demanded.

She snatched her arm away and came toward me again. "Please, Caleb." Suddenly she dropped to her knees as tears streamed down her face.

Any other time, that would've been all it took. Kendra had my heart on lockdown. Being with her had been pure heaven. She didn't work. I took care of all the bills, and she took care of me. I loved coming home to her. I looked at the dining room table. We had made love on it Saturday. I looked at the rug in front of the fireplace. Our bodies had become one on that rug. Every inch of this condo had been christened by our love.

My eyes made their way toward the bedroom—a bedroom bought by another man. The sex toys I bought were in the nightstand he bought. I had clothes in the dresser he bought.

Tears formed behind my eyelids as I realized my heaven had turned to hell.

"Baby, we're good together," Kendra whimpered, wiping her face. "I love you."

Tony, obviously disgusted by the sight of Kendra on her knees begging me to give her another chance, said, "Man, you can have this tramp."

"Naw, bruh. You need to take her with you," I said.

Kendra pulled herself up. "What?!"

"I said, get out."

She stared at me for a minute. "You can't put me out of my own house."

I looked around the room and saw my dad sitting over against the bar, obviously still in shock himself. He loved Kendra as if she were his own daughter. Shoot, she'd been the driving force that had brought us back together. I didn't have a relationship with him growing up, but she'd found him and got us to sit down and talk.

"Pops, hand me my bag. The one with my pistol in it. I'm about to blow somebody's brains out." I knew at that point I was probably just mouthing off, but if someone was to actually put a pistol in my hand, there was no telling what I would do.

"Fine," Kendra retorted as she pulled the belt of her robe tightly around her waist. "I'll leave tonight and give you some time to calm down. We'll talk tomorrow."

With that, she scurried off to the bedroom. But she was out of her mind if she thought we would be doing any talking at all.

Tony left, mumbling something about leaving before he "caught a case."

My dad must've known to give me my space because he retreated to the guest room, I guess to give me time to deal with my grief.

It took Kendra less than five minutes to change. She came out wearing a designer sweat suit, an overnight bag tossed across her shoulder.

She stopped right in front of me. "I'm sorry, baby." Lowering her eyes, she added, "But, um, look, I need your American Express to get a room."

I didn't know how to respond to that. So all I said was, "You need to get out of my face."

With that, she huffed and walked out the door. And for the first time since Tony came interrupting my tranquillity, destroying my perfectly constructed world, I sat down and let it all sink in. This time last year, I was going through the same thing with Vanessa after she used my American Express card to get her mother a breast job. Before that, it was Liza, who was still rolling around in the Mercedes I bought. I leaned my head back against the sofa, asking myself how the hell, once again, I had been gotten by a gold digger. How many times would I let some woman use me like this? I sighed in frustration. Just once I'd like to find a woman who loved me and not my money.

1

Paisley

There it was in black-and-white. My man, ass in the air, humping some ho in the back of *my* car.

I stared at the seven-inch video screen. The way the moonlight was shining down on the car and the way the lake glistened in the background made the whole scene look like something out of a romantic movie. But as the camera zoomed in on my fiancé all over some red-haired bimbo, I knew there was nothing romantic about what was going on.

Joe Gretzy's voice was calm, reassuring, like he was giving me the latest stock numbers. "Now, as you can see, he didn't waste any time taking her to the lakefront park, where he proceeded to—"

I cut him off. "I can see what he proceeded to do."

Joe nodded sympathetically as he fast-forwarded the tape. "This is the next day. Here's where we saw him pick the young lady up, then take her back to your apartment."

I bit my bottom lip and tried not to cry. "He took her to my apartment?"

"At least twice." Joe paused. "Are you okay?" he asked.

Like he really cared. The cameras were focused in on me, I'm sure, amplifying my tears, relishing my pain for the sake of ratings. But I'd come this far. I'd laid the foundation. I was so desperate to know if Bobby, who I'd been with for a year and a half, was cheating that I'd called the popular Houston-based reality show *Busted*. Right about now, I was both regretting that decision and glad I finally knew for sure. I'd suspected it, but Bobby always denied it. He would've kept denying it.

But there was no denying the videotape.

Joe picked up his cell phone, made a quick call, mumbled a few words, then snapped the phone shut.

"Right now, Bobby is at dinner with the girl in question. Are you ready to confront him?"

I thought about calling it off. Joe had made it clear that I could stop at any time, although I knew he didn't want me to. Besides, the cameras were positioned around me, poised for action.

Screw it. If they wanted action, I was about to give them action. I probably would've backed out if I hadn't known this whole being busted on TV thing would embarrass the hell out of Bobby. He was always trying to act hard in front of his boys. Let them see his ass get busted on national TV. Besides, after the day I'd had—I'd been fired from yet another job—I was ready to go off on somebody, and my cheating, no-good, dirty-dog boyfriend was the perfect target.

"Let's do this," I said, trying to keep my voice from cracking.

Joe gave the driver a hand signal and the white van took off. Luckily, we were less than five minutes from the restaurant where Bobby had taken his mistress-for-the-moment. I think the show planned it that way so I wouldn't have time to change my mind.

I tried to figure out how my life had come to this: breaking up on a stupid reality show.

"There he is. Let's go," Joe said as he jumped out of the van. I quickly followed suit.

I know I was supposed to wait for Joe to approach Bobby, but seeing him lean up against the railing with that fiery redheaded skank set me off. She was a smooth yellow tone color, looked like she'd been dipped in butter, with a small waist and legs that seemed like they stretched for miles. But it was the Dolly Parton breasts that made her stand out. That's probably what got Bobby's attention. He always was a breast man.

I took off running, throwing out my promise not to be one of those psycho women scorned I was always laughing at whenever I watched the show. Couldn't laugh at them anymore, because I was about to go straight Norman Bates.

I swung before I said a word. Bobby jumped and turned to face me, shock all over his face. "What the—?"

"You sorry piece of sh—." I swung again, this time connecting with the side of his face.

"Paisley!" He looked around at the three cameras and the soundman, all pointing their equipment at him. "What the hell is going on?"

"You tell me!" This Negro had the nerve to be wearing the linen shirt *I* bought for him.

Joe walked over and tried to talk to Bobby. "You wanna tell us why you're here, cheating on your fiancée?"

"Who the hell are you?" He turned toward the camera and pushed the lens. "Get that camera out of my face!"

Redhead covered her face.

"Don't hide. You wanna be out here creepin' with somebody else's man, be a woman about it!" I screamed.

"Paisley, what are you doing?" Bobby tried to grab my arm. I know he was trippin' over the whole scenario. This was totally out of character for me. But being crazy in love can make you crazy.

Joe stepped toward Bobby again. "We're with the TV show *Busted,* and *you've been busted.*"

"Cold busted, you no-good, trifling—" I swung again.

Bobby shot Joe an evil look. He started to say something, but then I guess decided he better focus his attention on me. "Paisley, let me explain."

"Explain what? How can you explain this?" I turned my fury to the redhead. "What—you can't get your own man?"

She shielded her face from the camera as she tried to grab her purse and take off. As she went toward one door, the camera followed. She went to another. The cameraman followed her there as well.

"Bobby, you'd better catch her, 'cause your ass needs a place to stay tonight. Naw, you need a place to stay permanently, for that matter."

"Please, don't do this. I need you."

I laughed in his face. "You should've thought about that before you decided to cheat on me." My anger was overtaking my pain. *Get it together, girl. You are above this.*

"Man, I'm not gon' tell you again. Get the camera out of my face!" Bobby pushed the cameraman so hard, he almost knocked the camera over.

By now, patrons in the restaurant were all outside, staring. Some were on their cell phones, no doubt giving their friends play-by-plays of the drama that was unfolding.

"I'm through! *We're* through." My voice was calm now. I was through acting the fool.

"No chance you all can work this out?" Joe asked.

This fool was about to work my nerves also. I had done what I'd come to do. It was time to go.

"No chance. At all. Can we get out of here?"

I headed back toward the van, trying to drown out Bobby's cries for me, while two of the *Busted* security guards tried to keep him away from me.

I climbed back in the van, holding my head high. Then I looked out the window at Redhead, who was speed walking down the street, away from the madness.

I had given Bobby's broke ass my heart. Shoot, I gave him my soul. Supported his dream to be a professional sports agent. Supported him every damn time things "just didn't work out." Worked two jobs so he could follow his dream. Worked two jobs so he could hobnob with athletes, hang out with the big dogs in hopes of making the "right connections." I did all that in the name of love. Tried to be everything to him, and it wasn't enough. I had even done a ménage à trois for him—and I don't even get down like that. But I wanted to please him.

My girlfriend Trina had tried to tell me this love stuff was for the birds. Trina is a what-have-you-done-for-me-lately type of girl. She used her Mary J. Blige good looks to get what she wanted from men. I used to think that was jacked up, but now I totally understood. If you didn't give them your heart, they couldn't break it.

No, I'd tried the love thing. I went against everything I believed in by being with Bobby. I had promised myself growing up that I would never date a broke man. I needed someone who could take me away from my life of poverty, but I threw that promise to the wind for Bobby. All because I was in love. *Screw love.* That was my motto from now on. Get what I can, while I can, then move on.

"Are you sure you're okay?" Joe asked as he climbed in the van.

"Just take me home, please." I closed my eyes and leaned against the seat as I thought about the next man in my life. He was going to have to bring it because if I was going to have my heart broken, I needed to at least get something out of the deal.

2

Caleb

For a year and a half, I'd been drama free. No women using me for my money. No discovering that some chick was playing me. No earth-shattering secrets. Just peace and tranquillity. And I think that's because of the woman on my arm, the woman I was madly in love with—Asia Murray.

Asia had come into my life and renewed my faith in love. I had kept my distance in the beginning, but she'd been patient, and now we had been together for over a year. I'd even asked her to marry me a month ago. But for some reason, I was starting to have doubts. I thought agreeing to travel sixty miles outside of Houston to Wharton, Texas, where her family was holding their annual reunion, might help ease my uneasy feelings.

Looking around, I was now wondering if that had been a good decision. That's because as we made our way up the sidewalk toward the pavilion, I felt like I had walked straight into the black Beverly Hillbillies' family reunion. That's the only way to describe the scene that was playing out before me.

A group of men were playing dominoes and arguing so loud,

I swear I thought somebody was about to start shooting. A group of older women stood off to the side, whispering like they were engaged in the best gossip in town.

My mouth fell open at a group of kids—they looked like they couldn't be any more than ten—dancing to "Bust It Wide Open."

I leaned into my girlfriend, Asia. "Do you all have any idea what that song is saying?"

She was bobbing herself. "Nope, not at all," she replied, like it was no big deal.

I stared at her in awe before saying, "He's talking about busting a girl wide open."

She laughed. "Boy, they're dancing to the beat. They're not paying attention to the words." She shook her head as she piled some ribs on her plate.

I looked back at the kids. Every single one of them was singing along. "Bust it wide open. B-B-Bust it wide open . . ." And the adults were standing around like that mess was cute.

I shook my head. Memo to self: *If I ever have kids with Asia, they will NOT be allowed to come to her family reunion.*

I met Asia at a happy hour at Grooves Restaurant & Lounge about a month after I broke up with Kendra. Asia was beautiful, and a lot plainer than the women I had been used to. I hadn't really been trying to talk to her, but we just fell into a natural rhythm conversing at the bar. We'd exchanged numbers, talked that night, and had been going strong ever since. But as much as I loved her, the doubts about our relationship weren't going away. And being here, watching her country relatives, definitely wasn't helping.

Following Asia, I filled my plate with all kinds of food that was sure to have my cholesterol skyrocketing. Then I took my plate and made my way to a picnic table, taking in all my surroundings. I couldn't believe my baby had come from this.

I sat off to myself for a while, watching Asia as she laughed with her people. She seemed oblivious to our deteriorating relationship. But truthfully, lately, she'd been doing and saying a lot of things that weren't sitting too well with me, making me rethink whether we really were right for each other.

"Baby, Pookie is gon' ride back with us because he's gon' stay with me for a few weeks."

Like that right there. Asia knew Pookie was a crackhead. He had stolen from everybody in the family. Why she would even entertain the notion that he should live with her for any amount of time was beyond me.

"Sorry, babe. Pookie ain't getting nowhere near my ride, and you the fool if you let him in your apartment to rob you blind." I was trying to be the voice of reason.

"That's family. He needs my help, and I'm gonna give it."

Memo to self: *Get my stuff out of her apartment.*

"Whatever, Asia." I popped the top on my grape soda and took a swig. We'd been at Asia's family reunion for about two hours now. And that was one hour and fifty minutes too long.

"What's up, Mr. Lawyer Man?" Asia's uncle Sam said as he sat down across from me.

"Actually, I'm an investment banker," I replied.

"Lawyer, investment banker. It's all the same."

"Really, it's not." I caught myself. Why was I arguing with a man who had a fifth-grade education?

I was grateful when Asia intervened. "Unc, are you giving my fiancé a hard time?"

"I'm just talkin' to the boy. Can't I talk to the boy?" Sam was a robust man who looked like he'd seen more than his fair share of trouble. He had a large scar under his right eye. His hair was thick on the sides and bald on the top.

Asia laughed and bit into a rib.

"So when y'all tying the knot?" Sam asked.

"In November," she replied.

"Umph. That's six months away. Sho is a long engagement."

"We're just making sure it's right," I said.

"Should've made sure of that before you agreed to marry each other."

I licked my lips. *Just let it go.* I flashed a fake smile.

"So, y'all gon' get a house? I bet y'all gon' be living all up in a mansion or something. Driving fancy cars. Shoot, Asia, you already rollin' like you Angela Bassett or something in that there fancy Camry."

I almost choked on my brisket.

"Yeah, Unc. My baby is gon' take good care of me." She squeezed my hand. "We haven't started house hunting yet, but I know my baby. He's gon' do it up big. I'm sure he's gonna have us in some four-bedroom, twenty-five-hundred-square-foot house or something."

"A freakin' mansion. I knew you had good taste, boy." Her uncle threw out a hearty laugh.

I looked at both of them to see if they were serious. They were.

Asia flashed me a warm smile. That smile is what captured my heart in the first place. Her deep dimples only accented it. I loved that about her. And I loved her long, wavy hair—evidence of the Trinidad in her blood.

After about twenty more minutes of Asia's ghetto-fabulous family, I'd had enough. "Hey, babe, you ready to roll?"

I could tell she wasn't really ready to go. But her gay cousin was over there shooting me funny looks and I needed to go before I hurt somebody.

"If you're ready, we can go."

"I'm ready." I was standing before she could finish her sentence.

We said our good-byes, which took a whole lot longer than I would've liked, but I breathed a sigh of relief once we were finally in my Range Rover, heading back to the city.

"Did you enjoy yourself?" Asia asked, shifting to get comfortable in the passenger seat.

I smiled but didn't answer.

She leaned back against the seat. "Uncle Sam has me thinking about our dream house. I can't wait until we get it."

"Ummm, speaking of that, were you for real about the four bedrooms?"

She shot me a concerned look. "Yeah. I hope I wasn't dreaming too big."

I chuckled. "Babe, come on. Twenty-five-hundred square feet? That's all you're shooting for?"

Her concerned look turned to an offended one. "What is that supposed to mean?"

I honked at the Ford Mustang driver who had cut me off. "I'm just saying," I continued, turning my attention back to her. "I'm trying to go to the top, not the middle."

"Well, excuse me if my little dreams don't fit into your big world." She folded her arms and stared out the window.

"I'm sorry, I wasn't trying to upset you. I didn't mean it."

"No, you said exactly what you meant. It's the same argument about me getting my master's degree."

I didn't want to go there with her again. I'd been trying to get her to go back to school to get that degree for six months now. I mean, how much did she expect to make as a teacher, getting a thousand-dollar pay raise only when the state legislature felt like giving her one?

"I was just trying to get you to see the bigger picture," I replied.

"I happen to like teaching." She was in a defensive mode now, and I was not in the mood to argue.

I sighed. "Fine, if you want to make thirty thousand dollars for the rest of your life, so be it."

"Everything is about money with you, Caleb. What about doing something fulfilling with your life? But I guess you wouldn't know anything about that."

"I'm very fulfilled. Shoot, I'm about to make partner at Abraham, Smith, and Cook. If that isn't fulfilling, I don't know what is."

"Would you do it for free?"

I looked at her as if she had lost her mind. "What?"

"Would you work at your job for free?"

"Hell, naw."

"Then you're not living your passion. Me, I would teach for free."

"You almost *are* teaching for free."

"Whatever, Caleb." She rolled her eyes. "Just take me home."

How did I end up arguing anyway? I was horny as hell, and judging by the disgusted look on her face, I wasn't going to see no parts of Miss Kitty tonight.

"Babe—"

"Caleb, just take my mediocre-dreaming, low-achieving self home."

"Babe—"

"*Home*, Caleb."

I sighed in frustration as I took the exit toward Asia's home.

3

Caleb

"What's up, blue balls?"

"Oh, you got jokes." I cut my eyes at my boy Todd, who was taking pleasure in my frustration with Asia. I'd called him after I dropped her off. I vented that not only was I horny but I was also tired of this same old argument.

Pushing past him, I made my way into his elaborately decorated condo. Todd was my best friend since the sixth grade, my boy who had my back and who rode me every chance he got.

"I told yo' ass that girl isn't in your league." He closed the door and followed me in.

"*That girl* is goin' to be my wife."

"Not if you got any sense, she won't be. I mean, come on, let's keep it real. The only reason you got with her in the first place is because she's safe and you were trying to make sure you didn't hook up with any more gold diggers. You knew Asia wasn't after you for your money. And guess what, it still wasn't enough for you." Todd walked over to his refrigerator, opened it, and pulled out two Heinekens. "Want one?"

I took it, popped the top, and almost downed it in one gulp.

"I'm just saying," he continued after he'd taken a sip of his beer, "you about to be a partner, patna. I mean, the big time. You need a dime on your arm."

"I guess like you," I said, motioning toward a picture on his end table of him and two busty, bikini-clad women.

"Yeah, like your boy here." He looked at the picture and licked his lips. "You can't tell me Miss Bud and Miss Bud Light aren't dimes. And once they pop those tops off, they're quarters."

I shook my head. Todd was forever the playa and took pride in it. The sad part was the women knew he was a playa and that only made them want him more.

"Asia is beautiful," I said as I sat down on his Italian leather sofa.

He picked up the remote and snapped the mute button on ESPN. "Asia is average. Don't get me wrong, you know I like her. She's really *sweet*." He put emphasis on "sweet." "But she's beautiful in an average sort of way. She's not Halle Berry or Michael Michele beautiful, but more like Kimberly Elise beautiful."

"That's the stupidest thing I ever heard," I quipped. "Kimberly Elise is gorgeous."

"But when you think dime, you think Halle, don't front. And I'm not saying there's anything wrong with average women. But man, you're Caleb Peterson, investment banker extraordinaire, soon-to-be-partner, six-figure, Range-Rover-sport-driving Caleb Peterson. I mean, come on, you'll be all over the celebrity accounts once you make partner, rollin' to places like the BET Awards and all the VIP stuff. You need a fly-ass girl rollin' with you."

I knew Todd was going off on one of his tangents, but I just needed someone to talk to. "What about marriage and children?"

"Man, miss me with that. You're thirty-one. You lucked up and ain't got nobody pregnant. You're a commodity, my brother. Marriage and children will be there whenever you want it. But take some time and enjoy those six figures, that top-notch position, and all the perks that come with it."

"So you think I should break up with Asia?"

"You should've been done broke up with Asia. I mean, damn. Can you imagine y'alls' wedding? Your side of the church got people like Quincy Jones. Her side has Uncle Sam and the Beverly Hillbillies." Todd shook his head like the thought alone was too much.

I wasn't one of those people who were easily influenced by their boys, but honestly, Todd wasn't saying anything I hadn't been thinking. I had an MBA from Princeton, I made one hundred and fifty thousand dollars a year, and I damn sure wasn't about to be happy with a four-bedroom house.

"So how do you suggest I break up with her?"

"I know you. You're a coward. You try to get her over and talk to her, she'll break out the crocodile tears, and next thing you know, y'all will be heading to the justice of the peace."

I laughed. Todd was right. I wouldn't be able to break it off with her face-to-face. "Maybe I can write her a letter."

"Man, this ain't no Lifetime movie. I know you think you all poetic and stuff, but a letter ain't the answer."

Todd broke out in a huge smile. "I have just the thing to make breaking up with Asia real easy."

He always had a plan. I sighed, not knowing if I really wanted to hear this. "How?"

"Make her hate you."

I turned up my lip. "I ain't trying to hurt her, man."

"Look," Todd leaned up like he was trying to talk sense into me, "you know Asia is your weakness, and you know anything less than her hating you ain't gon' work. If you try to talk to her, she's gonna cry or talk you out of it. If she hates you, she won't try to work things out; she won't try to get you to stay."

"Man, I don't know."

Todd leaned back. "Or you could just marry Asia, get you a little vinyl-siding home built in Fifth Ward, enroll your kids in a ghetto Houston school, and live happily ever after." He pressed the volume button and the sounds of Stuart Scott filled the room.

I thought about what he was saying. I really didn't want to hurt Asia. I loved her. I just was getting to the point where I didn't see us actually making it in a marriage. We had grown in two different directions. I sat, letting the thoughts simmer in my head for a few minutes.

Suddenly my cell phone vibrated. I glanced at it. Asia's soft face framed my screen. Closing my eyes, I answered. "Yeah?"

"I'm sorry, baby," she said quietly. "I didn't mean to get upset."

I felt my heart weakening. Asia always had a way of doing that to me. I imagined her big brown eyes with that puppy-dog look. She was probably twirling her finger around a strand of her hair, a nervous habit. But what made Asia so sweet is also what I was coming to despise. I knew no matter what we argued about, she would call me back within twenty-four hours, apologizing whether she was wrong or not.

Forever the peacekeeper. I wanted her to challenge me. Tell me to go to hell and not take my calls for three days. Make me come groveling back to her sometimes. Anything. But old, sweet, predictable Asia was on my phone, once again apologizing. Once again, giving in.

"You forgive me?" she asked.

I inhaled. Forgive her? It was always about forgiving her. "You know what, Asia? I don't feel like doing this with you. I'll holla at you later."

I rolled my eyes at Todd, who was shaking his head.

"We can get whatever size house you want," she continued. "I mean, I can only imagine what the electric bill would be on a big ol' house, but if that's what you want . . ."

I sighed. "Look, Asia, I'm at Todd's. He needs to talk. I'll call you later, okay?"

Silence.

"Okay," she finally said. "Caleb?"

"Yeah?"

"I love you."

"Yeah, a'ight. I'll talk to you later." I snapped the phone shut and let out a frustrated breath.

Todd cut his eyes at me, then handed me a piece of paper.

"What's this?" I said, taking it.

"Miss Bud Light's number. Tell her you're a friend of mine. She'll make you forget all about Asia. Just make sure Asia walks in while she's helping you forget."

I stared at Todd for a minute. I couldn't believe I was even contemplating something like this. But Asia's face popped up in my head again with images of me trying to break it off and losing courage. Images of an unmatched future.

Then my phone beeped. I looked down. A text message from Asia with two little words: *I'm sorry*.

As bad as it sounded, maybe Miss Bud Light was the answer. I sighed as I programmed the number into my phone.

4

Paisley

I hate men. Every single one of their no-good, lying, cheating, dirty asses.

I hated the man at the cleaners who, despite the wedding ring on his finger, was trying his best to mack on the pretty young thing who'd come in to drop off her clothes. I even hated the damn doorman who was looking at me right now as if I were a juicy pork rib and he wanted to suck all the meat off my bone.

"May I help you?" I snapped as we walked in the building.

"I'm sorry, I thought you were that actress Gabrielle Union."

I rolled my eyes. I got that a lot and although we looked a little alike, I was cuter. Anyway, that look the doorman was giving me wasn't because he thought I was some celebrity. He was looking like he wanted to jump my bones.

The doorman looked away, embarrassed.

My girlfriend Brenda cut her eyes at me. "Dang, would you chill out?"

"Whatever." I waved her off. "Why are we coming over to Trina's? I told you, I'm ready to go home."

"And I told you, Trina asked us to stop by and help her with something," Brenda said, reaching over and ringing the doorbell.

Trina swung the door open. "What's up? What's up? What's up?" she sang. "Y'all ready to get your party on?"

I could hear the music thumping in the background. I rolled my eyes and turned to Brenda. "Why is it so difficult for you to follow instructions?" I asked, letting her know I wasn't in the mood to be playing. "I specifically said I wasn't in the mood to party."

Brenda shrugged and flashed her gap-toothed smile. "I didn't have anything to do with it. I was just following instructions to get you here. I've done my part." She walked off before I could say another word.

"Chill out and leave that funky attitude at the door."

I turned to my best friend, Trina, who was standing there with a bottle of Alizé in one hand and a cigarette in the other.

Quickly sucking my teeth, I walked past her and into her living room, which was illuminated with a strobe light. I looked at the light, then at her.

"What?" she shrugged. "We're about to party for real."

I released an exasperated breath and set my purse down on her coffee table. It was useless to argue with Trina when she was ready to party.

Brenda and I had just come back from the hair salon, where I had struggled to make my way through my session without folks getting all up in my business. It wasn't easy, with Shyla asking what was wrong every two minutes, but I managed to do okay. It was almost eight o'clock when we finally pulled out of there. I was mad, but being in there did help take my mind off Bobby.

"Look, I'm about to just go to the house and chill. I told you I didn't want to go out after we left the shop."

Trina popped the top on the bottle and poured some of the Alizé into a wineglass. "Let's get this party started."

I sighed in frustration. In addition to Brenda, there were four of our other friends there, stretched out on Trina's sectional.

I was just about to say something when I looked at the fireplace. "What in the world . . . is that?" I said, taking a step toward the fireplace.

"What does it look like?" Trina laughed.

"Why do you have a poster-size picture of Bobby?" I leaned in closer. "And is that a . . . Is that a *penis* in his ear?"

"Yvette drew that, with her nasty ass." Brenda laughed. "But you have to admit, the likeness is amazing. So real, so three-dimensional."

I was trying not to laugh. "Why did you draw a penis in Bobby's ear?" I asked Yvette.

She shrugged. "I thought since we can't chop it off for real, I could at least pretend."

I chuckled. "Y'all stupid," I said as I took the glass of Alizé.

Trina handed me a marker as well. "Your turn."

"Whatever." I decided to just try to chill and enjoy the evening. *No sense in spending another night depressed,* I thought as I plopped down on the sofa next to Yvette and took in Trina's wall-to-wall entertainment console. It was made of a shiny cherrywood and housed a large HD plasma TV screen. Everything was brand-spanking-new, not to mention expensive looking.

"Dang, girl, I didn't know you redecorated," I said as I took in the new coffee tables. "This must've cost you a grip."

"It didn't cost her a thing, except a few hours of work on her back." Brenda snickered and gave Trina a high five.

I loved her to death, but Trina was the ultimate gold digger. It's like she smelled money, and when she spotted a man with looks and money, it wouldn't take her but a minute and he'd be at the Galleria buying her whatever she wanted.

As the videos played on BET, I tried to keep my mind from going back to Bobby. He'd been calling me nonstop since Friday, when I'd busted him.

The doorbell rang, and since Trina had walked in the kitchen and neither Brenda nor Yvette looked like they were going to make a move, I went to answer it.

I pulled the door open and stepped aside as Trina's cousin Nay-Nay and two other girls came strolling in.

"Hey, Paisley, this is Kim and Tanya," she said as they strolled in.

"Party over here!" one snapped and even stopped to shake her barely covered behind in the coochie cutters she was sporting.

I had just closed the door when someone else knocked. I opened the door again, and there stood the prettiest dark chocolate man I had ever seen in my life. He had a washboard stomach with bulging biceps and thick legs that poked out through his bad imitation of a firefighter's uniform. And damn, he was fine!

I couldn't hide the smile that curled at my lips.

"I'm Eric, the extinguisher," he said and pulled the waistband to his pants. They snapped against that six-pack so loud, everyone started fanning themselves.

"I heard there was a fire in this apartment." Eric flashed us his sexy smile and I all but wanted to melt.

"You damn straight there's a fire up in here!" Nay-Nay giggled.

"And we need your fine self to do something about it," her friend Kim added.

Someone changed the music, and Eric didn't waste any time moving to the middle of the living room floor.

When the music started blasting, we were all up, trying to make a sandwich out of Eric. He was loving every minute of it.

"The roof, the roof, the roof is on fire!" Brenda screamed.

"We don't need no water, 'cause Eric ain't gonna let it burn!" Nay-Nay yelled.

I swear it was like a big freak show up in there as we were all jockeying for position on Eric. I know I personally was hanging on to his chest. He made it bounce each time I squeezed his nipple. Finally he got a break when the doorbell rang again.

I think it was Trina who went to get the door. Just then, Eric looked up from between my legs. I'm not quite sure how he got there, but when he saw the other women strolling in, he had a look of alarm on his face and I thought we had scared the man away.

"I'll be right back," he said. Over his shoulder, he asked, "Where's your bathroom?"

"Back there to your right. What do you need?" Trina asked, wearing a worried look on her own face.

"Baby, this is a three-alarm fire. I need to call for some backup." He disappeared down the hall.

"Ooooh weeee, it's getting hot in heerre," someone yelled.

I didn't quite know how to thank Trina, but two hours into my so-called pity party, I wasn't even thinking anymore about Bobby or the fact that I'd been fired from my job. I stood in the kitchen drinking Alizé and munching on vegetables from the platters. By the time it was all said and done, Eric had called two more of his boys, then they brought along a couple of friends, and we had a real bona fide party going on. When I say no one was feeling pity, I'm sure I'm not speaking for just myself.

"This party is too crunk!" Nay-Nay said as she hobbled into the kitchen where I was standing. As she looked over at me, I was glad Trina had decided to try to cheer me up.

The party went on until three in the morning. And I can't be sure, but I think I saw Nay-Nay and her girls leave out of there with one of Eric's friends. He did, however, pass out his cards to us all and swore he'd break us off a huge discount the next time someone lost a man or just wanted to have some fun.

I didn't even try to make it back to my apartment. I was barely walking straight when I closed the door on the last person who said they were heading out.

"Girl, that party was off the chain," Tanya said as she eased on out the door.

"Trina, girl, this was just what I needed," I said after everyone was gone. Trina looked at me like she was barely able to keep her eyes open, and I thoroughly understood. I wanted nothing more than to fall off to sleep and not be bothered unless the place really was on fire.

5

Caleb

I shouldn't be doing this. My head was telling me this was not the answer. But my other head was saying, "Shut up and let her ride you."

And boy, was Miss Bud Light riding me. Like we were in the Kentucky Derby, and I was a champion stallion.

Water and Melon, as she affectionately called her forty-two double Ds, were bouncing up and down, nearly giving me a concussion. I laughed when she told me her pet names for her breasts and wanted to tell her that was the corniest thing I'd ever heard. But right about now, she could call those bad boys whatever she wanted because I was about to go picnicking.

I dove in, burying my face between her breasts, which actually were the size of two watermelons. She bounced up and down as she moaned, "Oooh, daddy, just like that."

It had been a long time since I'd had sex like this. I mean, I had been faithful to Asia since we got serious. And while the sex was good with her, it was nothing like this. It was usually just the standard missionary, boring position.

No, sex with Asia never felt so good.

So why was I feeling so bad?

Probably because I knew Asia was on her way over here. Probably because I truly loved Asia and didn't even know Miss Bud Light's real name. Probably because even though I wanted out, I didn't want to hurt Asia.

I squirmed, feeling myself losing my erection. How could I possibly be losing my erection?

"Wait," I said, trying to ease her bouncing.

She looked at me like I was crazy. "Wait for what?" she asked, finally stopping.

"Just wait." I was getting limper by the minute. "I can't do this." I eased her off of me.

"You've got to be kidding me, right?" She had this look like no man had ever dared stop having sex with her, let alone *before* he came.

"I'm sorry. . . . What's your name again?"

"Alizé," she said with a wicked grin.

"Is that your real name? What your mama named you?"

She looked at me like, why did I need to know that?

"It's Chante."

I stared at Chante's beautifully bought body. The double Ds now screamed implants. The face looked like it had seen more than its share of Botox sessions, and several horses had definitely died in order for her to sport that wild, honey-colored hairdo.

She may be Miss Bud Light, but Asia was my Heineken.

Asia, in all her simplicity, in all her realness. That was who I wanted. That was who I couldn't stop thinking about. Yes, we had some issues, but right then and there I decided they were worth working through.

"Look, Chante. I'm sorry. I'm just not feeling this." I stood and looked around for my underwear.

"Come again?"

I handed her her bra, which looked like two cannonball slingshots.

"I . . . just can't do this."

She took her bra, the dumbfounded look still across her face. "I thought you wanted to kick it. Todd said you wanted to take me places I'd never been before." She reached up and rubbed my chest.

Somehow I doubted there was any place she hadn't been.

"I do. I mean, I did." I removed her hand. "I mean, I just . . . I was just trying to get my girl to leave me. Figured if she caught me, she'd hate me, and it would be so much easier to break up. But I can't do it like this. Don't even know if I want to do it at all."

She frowned as she began fastening her bra. "Ooooh, a playa with a conscience."

I stepped into my clothes. "I'm sorry. You're a beautiful woman. But I love my girl. This is stupid."

I couldn't believe I'd let Todd talk me into this foolishness.

She stood and slipped her thong on, then shook her head as she pulled her minidress back over her head. "If you love her so much, why are you here with me?"

"That's the question I've been asking myself all night."

She stared blankly at me for a few minutes before she reached down and grabbed her purse.

I quietly followed her to the door and could tell she had an attitude.

When I opened the door, she stepped out into the hallway, then spun toward me. "You could've at least let me come. Now I have to go home all horny and stuff."

"I'm sorry, Chante."

She rolled her eyes. "Look here, Caleb. The next time you want to use someone to try and get your girl to break up with you, don't call me."

"I'm sorry—"

"You right, you're sorry. That itty-bitty thang you're sporting is sorry." She pointed at my crotch. "And I'm sorry I ever came over here to see your sorry ass."

I know she didn't call Mr. Charlie itty-bitty.

"And to think I turned down another dude for this. I would've been better off using my damn vibrator." She spun off. "Sorry bastard."

I was just about to say something to her when I looked at the edge of the steps that led to my second-floor condo. I thought I would die as I watched Asia stand there with tears warming her cheeks.

"Oh no," I mumbled.

She turned and took off down the stairs. I bolted after her. "Baby, wait." I stopped her just as she reached her car. "Please, let me explain."

With the exception of the tears streaming down her face as she stood there, Asia was remarkably calm as she turned around. "There's nothing to explain, Caleb." She took a deep breath. "You wanted out." She paused. "You wanted out so badly, you would go through this." She motioned toward my half-clad body. "Well, you got it. You're out."

"No, Asia. I mean, I thought I wanted out. I just didn't know how to break it off."

She laughed. It was a hollow, pained laugh. "You could have sent a freaking e-mail, Caleb."

I was speechless.

"Please give me a chance to explain."

She looked at me with pity now. "I don't understand you, Caleb. Do you want out or not?"

"No. Yes. I mean . . . ughhhh!" I know I wasn't making sense.

"Look, Caleb." She wiped her eyes and tossed her hair out of her face. "Let me help you out." She reached down and eased the three-carat solitaire off her left hand. "When you gave me this, I told you I would've been happy with a band. I didn't need anything fancy. I just wanted you. A lifetime with you. But I've come to the slow realization that I can never be enough for you." Then she gently set it in my hand. "The fact that you would stoop so low as to sleep with another woman in hopes that I would catch you and leave you is just, well . . . words can't even describe how ludicrous that is. And you know what? I deserve better than that."

"I realized it was stupid. That's why I stopped."

"And that's supposed to make me feel better?" She shook her head as she sat down in the driver's seat. Starting the car, Asia rolled down the window. "Caleb, I will always love you, but you are pathetic. And I deserve better than you."

With that, Asia backed up and drove away, leaving me standing in the middle of the parking lot, feeling like I'd just made the biggest mistake of my life.

6

Caleb

"*E'rebody at the club . . .*"

The music was thumpin'. Bodies were jumpin'. The crowd was hype.

And I'd rather have been anywhere else.

I leaned over to Todd. "I'm out." Then I turned and headed to the door before he could say another word.

Todd muttered a curse word and quickly took off after me, catching me just as I stepped outside the door.

"Man, what is your problem? You been in a funk since we got here, and we haven't been here more than an hour. You all up in the club, looking like a brokenhearted teenager." He shook his head at me. "I'ma need you to snap outta this. I don't take depressed brothers nowhere with me."

I felt myself getting upset. "That's why I told you to leave me at home."

"Negro, please. You been in the house, sulking like a little bitch for a week now."

"Man, I got your bitch." I couldn't appreciate Todd trying to play me like that.

"Chill, don't be gettin' all sensitive. I'm just saying, you done called the girl fifty-eleven times and she ain't hearing it. You've stalked her at work, at home. Called her mama and the rest of her country, ghettofied kinfolk. Nobody's hearing you, man. Let it go. Let it go before she gets a restraining order on your ass." He brushed some lint off my jacket. "And let's go up in this party and meet some *African* queens so you can forget all about your *Asian* princess."

"Man, listening to you is how I got in this predicament in the first place." I know I was whining, but I couldn't ease the ache in my heart. It was surprising; I never knew how strongly I felt about Asia until she was gone. And the fact that I'd hurt her, hurt me that much more.

Todd pulled me out of the way of a black Infiniti that came barreling toward us. Then he turned and screamed at the driver. "Slow your ass down! You're in a freakin' parking lot!"

The driver shot us the finger and kept going.

Todd shook his head and turned back to me. "That's why women shouldn't be allowed on the road. Anyway, as I was saying, I don't understand you. You the one came over to my house, crying because you wanted to get rid of your girl. You've been complaining about her nonstop for the last three months. Now she's gone. That's what you wanted, so what's the problem?"

"I just didn't know it would hurt so bad," I softly murmured.

"Please don't ever say no sissy crap like that again." Todd stopped and looked at a group of women as they made their way into the club. "How are you beautiful ladies doing this evening?"

The women giggled and waved as they walked inside.

Todd turned back to me. "Okay, therapy session over. Let's go."

"I'm out, I told you."

He shot me a sly smile. "And just how would you be getting out? I drove, remember?" He laughed, turned around, and made his way back inside.

I took a deep breath. This was exactly why I didn't like rolling somewhere without my own ride. I tried to shake off the melancholy cloud that hung over my head. Might as well do like Todd said and try to let it go. Asia was adamant. It was over.

I followed him back inside. He was nowhere to be found, so I headed to the VIP room, where I spent the next hour downing the free drinks.

The club was wall-to-wall packed. It was a private party being given by one of the Houston Texans, and the women were out in full effect.

Navigating my way through the crowd, I was just about to turn down the hall that led to the VIP room when I spotted the most beautiful woman I'd ever seen, the type that will make you do a 360-degree turn four times. She was standing at the bar nursing an apple martini, looking like she'd also rather be anyplace else. Her golden-brown hair flowed down her back. It looked like the ocean, and I just wanted to dive straight in. From where I stood, her skin looked flawless. My eyes made their way up and down her five-foot-six frame. She had just enough meat on her bones to make her fine, and every ounce of her body was proportioned just right. Unlike the other hoochies in the club, she was dressed classy in a hunter green wrap top and some black capris that were so tight, her pores had to be choking. She wore black three-inch-heel sandals with straps that wrapped around her perfectly sculpted legs.

I suddenly felt myself perking up. So I exhaled, then shook off any sadness I was feeling as I made my way over to her.

"So that's why it rained today," I said as I approached her.

"Excuse me?" she responded.

"I said, that's why it rained today. God was crying because He'd lost one of His angels."

She stared blankly at me. "Does that really work on anyone?"

I smiled. Women sometimes had a hard time understanding my poetic expressions. Not to be dismayed, I extended my hand. "I'm Caleb. Caleb Peterson."

She looked down at my hand, but didn't take it. "I'm not interested."

I could see this one wasn't going to be easy. "Neither am I, really."

She looked taken aback.

"No, I didn't mean it like that." I looked around the club, decided to step out of my mack mode and just be myself. "I came over to talk to you because you seem 'bout like me and would rather be anyplace else."

She gave me a look like I had her pegged.

"Me and my girl broke up, and my friend dragged me over here, trying to help me get over it," I said, motioning for the bartender. "Can I get some Hennessy and another apple martini for the lady?" I looked at her to make sure that was all right. She nodded that it was.

After that, she scooted next to me at the bar. "Sounds like you're in the same boat as me. My girlfriends dragged me here too." She took a deep breath. "I'm Paisley."

I smiled. "Beautiful name. Are you from Houston?"

She nodded. "Born and raised."

"Married?"

"Nowhere near. Just caught my fiancé cheating, so very much single."

I cringed at that. An image of Asia telling some other man that same thing flashed through my mind, but I quickly shook it off.

"Kids?" I asked as the bartender slid us our drinks. I slid him a twenty and motioned for him to keep the change.

Paisley took her drink. "Nope, and what's with the twenty questions?"

I shrugged. "Just asking."

Paisley and I made our way over to a small table, where we sat and talked for another hour. Todd had spotted me, given me the thumbs-up, and then disappeared.

Our conversation was interrupted when a woman dressed in what looked like red lingerie sashayed over to our table.

"Girl, there you are. I thought you had bailed on us." The woman was very attractive, but her ghetto demeanor was unappealing. And the way she was smacking on that gum made her look cheap.

"Hey, Trina. I've just been sitting over here, making small talk."

Trina, who finally noticed me, looked me up and down. "Umph. And you would be—?"

"Hi, I'm Caleb."

"What do you do?" she asked as she leaned back and scanned my body.

"Excuse me?"

She put her hands on her hips. "I didn't stutter."

"Trina!" Paisley snapped.

"What?" Trina turned her lips up. "All these busters in here, ain't no need in you wasting your time."

Paisley shook her head. "You'll have to excuse my friend."

"You don't have to excuse nothing," Trina said. "I'm just keeping it real. If he knew you worked at McDonald's, he wouldn't be wasting time sitting up here talking to you."

I looked at Paisley. "You work at McDonald's?"

She laughed. "No, she's kidding. I'm actually in between jobs."

"But see, that proves my point," Trina said triumphantly.

"Well, I'm an investment banker."

"Ooooh. Carry on," she laughed.

I smiled, hoping she was just playing, but somehow I didn't think she was.

After Trina walked off, I turned back to Paisley. "I'd really like to call you sometime."

Paisley suddenly lost her smile. "You know, Caleb, I've really enjoyed talking to you, but I have to be honest. I'm just not in the dating mood right now."

I reached in my pocket and pulled out a business card, then handed it to her. She reluctantly took it. "Here, take my card. It has my cell on it. We don't have to date. We can be friends." I took in her beauty. Even in the dim light of the club, I could tell she was absolutely stunning.

Paisley ran her fingers through her hair, looked me up and down like she really liked what she saw, but then said, "Caleb, as enticing as that sounds, I have enough friends. Take care." She stood and managed a smile before turning and walking off.

I watched the elegant way she exited, taking comfort in the fact that despite what she'd said, she still had dropped my card in her purse.

7

Paisley

I don't know why I couldn't get that man off my mind. I'd been thinking about Mr. Caleb Peterson since the party last week. He'd definitely made an impact on me, but I just didn't want to get caught up in another man, so I pushed thoughts of Caleb aside.

"Ouch!" I flinched as my hairdresser, Shyla, let the steam from the curling iron get too close to my neck.

"Sorry," Shyla said. "I was all caught up in Trina's story. Finish, girl."

I rolled my eyes at their gossiping behinds. Trina was filling Shyla, Keri, and the other stylists in on her latest escapade, some guy she'd suckered into paying off her credit cards.

"Damn, I wanna be like you when I grow up," Keri said.

"Hey, what can I say?" Trina replied as she picked up two magazines from the coffee table.

I laughed. "Hand me that *Black Enterprise*," I said.

Trina tossed the magazine to me.

"Did you tell Shyla about that fine guy you met at the club?" Trina asked as she flipped open a *Jet* magazine.

I threw her a look to get her to shut up. She knew I hated having Shyla all up in my business.

"Girl, 'bout time you met somebody to help you get over Bobby," Shyla said.

"I did not *meet* anyone to help me get over Bobby," I protested. "It's just some guy I sat with and talked to at the club, that's all."

Trina turned up her lip. "Sat up *all* night with."

I shook my head and started flipping through my magazine. "Trina just doesn't get the fact that I'm done with guys for a minute. Can't take the heartache."

"Girl, they gon' give you heartache whether you deal with them now or later," Keri cackled.

I was about to say something when a huge photo on page twenty-six of the magazine caught my eye. My mouth fell open. "Oh. My. God."

Trina sat up. "What?"

I blinked my eyes, trying to make sure I wasn't just seeing things, then I looked at the name. Yep, that was him.

I held up the magazine toward Trina. "Do you know who that is?"

Trina squinted at the magazine, reading the headline. "'Brothers Making Bank.' Umphh. Looks like somebody I need to know."

I pushed the magazine toward her. "Look closer. It's the guy from the club. Caleb Peterson."

"Oh, snap!" Trina jumped up and snatched the magazine. "It sure is." She started reading. "'Investment banker Caleb Peterson is among those brothers under thirty-five making their mark in the financial arena. Peterson is an investment banker with the firm Abraham, Smith, and Cook.' Girl, if you don't want him, I'll take him," Trina said as she licked her lips.

"Would you shut up and finish reading," Shyla snapped. She'd stopped doing my hair, and like everyone else in the salon was focused intently on Trina.

"All right, all right," she continued. "'Peterson is poised to make junior partner, which will make him the first African American to hold such a high-ranking position with the century-old firm. Abraham, Smith, and Cook boasted receipts totaling two point three billion dollars last year.'" She looked up at me. "Good God Almighty."

Shyla pulled my hair. "Did she say *billion*?"

"Billion, baby," Trina responded.

"Daaaamn. I don't even know how many zeros that is," Keri chimed in.

"It's not like Caleb is getting the billions. The company is," another customer interjected.

Trina looked at her like, who the hell was she? "Regardless, from the sound of this article, he's getting some of that money." She turned back to me. "Girl, I didn't know he had it going on like that."

"Me neither," I replied. My mind started replaying what I had done with his business card. I think I'd tossed it as soon as I got home.

"So when are y'all going out?" Shyla's voice interrupted my thoughts.

"Ummm, we're not," I replied.

"What do you mean, you're not?" Trina asked.

"I threw his card away."

Trina slapped her forehead. "Good grief, Paisley! Have I not taught you *anything*?" She shook the magazine at me. "This man is loaded. You are sitting at home. Your savings are about to run out. You have no prospects of a job. You're about to get evicted because you can't pay your rent. And you're wallowing in pity, and I saw it in his eyes—he was feeling you."

I sighed, not even dealing with the fact that Trina had just put all my business on Front Street. Caleb was great conversation. But I needed a little more time before I got involved with another man. Or did I?

"'Brothers Making Bank,'" Trina said. "That's what he is—a brother making bank. Not some two-bit, two-timing dreamer. You betta call him."

"Well, I couldn't even if I wanted to. Did you not hear me say I threw his business card away?"

Trina shook her head as she popped out her cell phone, punched in some numbers, and waited. "Yes. Houston. I need the number for Abraham, Smith, and Cook." She hesitated. "Umm-huh. Got it." She scribbled the number down, then handed me both the phone and the paper. "Call him."

I stared at the phone. Although I liked this guy, I had to ask myself, would I be calling him if I hadn't seen this article?

Trina must've been reading my mind. "Didn't you say you were all about getting yours after that mess with Bobby? Didn't you say you were through with broke men? Well, Caleb looks anything but broke. Call him, girl."

I hesitated. Caleb was handsome, well built, and it definitely looked like he had money—all the qualities I said the next guy was going to have. Smiling, I took the phone from Trina and dialed his number.

8

Caleb

I was in shock as I held the phone. I couldn't believe Paisley had actually called, especially since she'd seemed adamant that she wasn't interested. But who was I to question divine intervention?

My secretary, Dedra, stood in my office, no doubt trying to be nosy and see who it was I was talking to. She started playing with her chestnut brown hair with one hand and placed the other hand on her hip, her way of telling me she didn't want to leave. She playfully rolled her eyes as I waved her out of the room.

This was just the icing on my cake of a day. I'd brokered two major deals, both of which would put a hefty commission in my pocket. I made a mental note to give Dedra her share because she was the glue that held my office together.

I didn't want to seem too eager, like I'd been waiting for Paisley's call, so I hesitated. "Who is this again?" I asked as I leaned back in my leather chair.

"Oh, you met that many women at the club that you can't remember who I am?" Her voice was soft and sultry, like a smooth Teddy Pendergrass song.

I let out a small laugh. "Naw, it ain't even like that."

"This is Paisley. We sat and talked for over an hour Saturday night."

"Oh, the 'I'm not interested' beautiful young woman I spent most of the night with?"

"That would be me."

We talked about nothing in particular for a few minutes before I turned the conversation to what I really wanted to know. "So tell me, Miss Paisley, why doesn't a lovely lady like yourself have a man?"

"Who said I didn't?"

That caused me to sit up in my seat. "Excuse me?"

"I'm just kidding. I'm very much single. As I told you at the club. Me and my boyfriend broke up four months ago. I left him."

I wanted to ask what he did to make her leave, but luckily, she answered before I had to.

"We were together for a year," she continued. "He just could never get it together, was always chasing empty dreams. But the final straw was the fact that he had another woman on the side. Had her the whole time. Probably had a bunch of women."

I couldn't help but notice how her voice went down an octave.

"It took you that long to figure out that fool was no good?" I said, trying to lighten the mood.

I looked up at Dedra, who was back standing in my office, pointing at her date book and the clock. "Your meeting starts in an hour, and we still have to go over this," she mouthed as she held up a folder.

Damn. My conversation with Paisley was going so good, but this meeting was important because they were talking about naming me as a junior partner next week. So I needed to review some notes before I headed into it.

"Look, Paisley, as much as I would love to sit here and talk with you all afternoon, I have a meeting I have to get to."

"Oh, what do you do again?"

"I'm an investment banker. Actually just made partner at my firm."

"Oh," she said, not really sounding impressed.

Dedra was still standing there, glaring at me. I swung around in my seat to keep her out of my business. "What are you doing this evening?" I asked Paisley.

"Ummm, nothing. Why? You got something in mind?"

"Dinner. Let me come pick you up and take you out to eat."

"I don't know you like that to let you come to my house. For all I know, you might be a serial killer," she joked.

"Well, meet me there then."

"Meet you where?"

"How about Timmy Chan's on MLK?"

"Excuse me?"

I laughed. "I'm just kidding. You don't strike me as the Timmy Chan type."

"I'm not." She said that with a laugh, but I could tell she wasn't joking.

"Let's meet at Chez Soul. I love that place, and they have a great jazz singer tonight."

"I'll see you at seven."

"Seven it is."

Reluctantly I hung up and faced Dedra, who was still standing there with her arms folded across her chest. "That didn't sound like Asia to me."

"Asia is history. I've moved up to someone more my caliber." I flashed a huge smile.

Dedra wasn't amused. "That's foul, Caleb. Asia was a sweet

girl. And I hope you don't get an even bigger head than you already have just because you're about to be a junior partner."

I stood up from my desk. "And don't forget about the forty-thousand-dollar pay raise."

"Whatever, Caleb. Just remember, you reap what you sow."

"Okay, now you sound like somebody's mama."

"I'm just telling you. I've been with you six years, and you know I'm going to keep it real."

"Well, can you keep it real—quiet and be gone?" I playfully waved her out.

Dedra walked toward the door, but stopped and turned to me. "Don't forget your brother is coming by here for you to meet his newest client, some singer named Sway."

I shook my head. My brother, Damon, was trying to be the next big music producer. He'd started a celebrity management company and was always looking for the next big star. The problem was, he didn't have a pot to piss in nor a window to throw it out of, and he always came to me to foot his bills.

"I forgot about that. What time is he coming?"

Dedra looked at her watch. "In about ten minutes."

I gave her a sly smile. "Why don't you stick around and deal with my brother? You know you have a way of charming him."

"Nope. Marcus and I are going to Vegas," she said, referring to her boyfriend.

"Oooh, you gon' finally give him some?" I had teased Dedra about her nerdy-looking boyfriend and the fact that they'd been together nine months and hadn't had sex.

"No. I told you, I'm serious about being celibate until I get married."

I laughed. "How noble. But more power to the brother. Couldn't be me."

"I know it couldn't, 'cause you'se a freak," she joked.

I started gathering my things. "And proud of it. But I'm 'bout to jet before Damon comes in here begging for money. We can go over the notes in the conference room." I shut down my computer and headed toward the door, squeezing Dedra's cheeks as I passed her on my way out.

9

Caleb

No wonder my mother couldn't keep a man. If she talked his ear off like she was doing mine right about now, I couldn't blame any man for not sticking around.

I sighed heavily as I listened to my mother ramble on about the hairdresser who didn't get her hair just right. Why she thought I wanted to hear this mess was beyond me.

But I knew my mother. If I tried to cut Marva Peterson off, it would only prolong the conversation. So I let her ramble in the hopes that she would wrap up soon. I didn't have to wait long.

"All right, baby. I know you're a busy man. But when are you going to come see me again?"

Maybe I should've gotten off the phone when I had the chance.

"Mama, don't start."

"Don't start what? I live less than twenty miles from you and your brother, and I never see either of you."

I hated having this discussion with my mother. I don't know why I didn't visit her much. Damon claimed it was because I still had issues with her because I couldn't get past her leaving us for a man when we were kids. I shook off that thought, not wanting to go down that road again. It had taken me a long time to work through my anger at my mother for putting her needs before her two young sons'.

"Mama, I will come see you this weekend, how's that?" I responded.

"Umm-hmmm, I'll believe it when I see it," she mumbled.

"Bye, Ma. I gotta go. Love you." I needed to get off before she started on another tirade. Plus, I just saw a vision of loveliness that had to be Paisley walk into the restaurant.

"Love you, too, Caleb."

I snapped my cell phone shut and quickly stepped out of my car.

Paisley stopped at the entrance to Chez Soul and looked around. She was absolutely gorgeous in a black, diamond-studded I AM Fashions T-shirt that read I AM a queen. Normally, I would've been turned off by a woman wearing a T-shirt on a first date, but the way it hugged her chest, there wasn't anything I could say. Besides, she had on a rust-colored cropped jacket, which made it look less casual. She also wore a pair of Blessed Jeans and some black-studded strappy sandals. In fact, she looked like she had just stepped off the pages of a fashion magazine.

I stood to the side for a moment, taking in her beauty, watching the men try to holla at her and the ease and style in which she shot them down.

Finally I made my way over to her. "Hey, beautiful."

"Hey, yourself." She smiled as she leaned in to hug me. The scent of jasmine penetrated my nostrils. Damn, I love a woman who smells good.

We made our way inside and got settled at our table. Over

dinner, we talked about everything under the sun. She shared with me how she had grown up dirt-poor and was determined that she would never go without again. She told me she had been a model for a short period, but the work had dried up. Up until a few weeks ago, she worked in customer service for a local telephone company. But she'd lost that job after getting into it with her supervisor.

I felt like Paisley opened up her soul to me as she told me about her brother dying when she was a senior in high school. She had begun telling me how, but then had gotten choked up and would only say that she blamed herself. I had even opened up to her about my issues with my mother. I think we both were surprised the conversation had taken such a deep turn, but it's like we just totally clicked.

Three hours later, when we were standing outside the restaurant, it was obvious neither of us wanted the night to end.

"So, are you about to head home?" she softly asked.

"Unless you can think of some better place for us to go," I replied.

"Is my place better?" she offered seductively.

Now that's what the hell I'm talking about. A woman who takes control and has no shame in her game. Women get all wrapped up in that "I don't want to sleep with him because he might think bad of me" mentality. It's the twenty-first century. I want to know if we're sexually compatible so I don't have to waste my time.

I looked Paisley up and down. Somehow I had no doubt we were sexually compatible. "Your place sounds lovely," I replied.

I followed her back to her apartment on the north side. It was a modest two-bedroom condo, but it was immaculate and seemed to fit her just right.

Paisley popped in a Big Luther CD, not one Luther made after he lost all of the weight but one of those sexy "make a woman do anything you want" songs.

I didn't waste any time. As soon as the music got to playing good, I moved in close to her. Then I leaned in to kiss her passionately and the next thing I knew, we were getting hot and heavy.

We were like two animals in heat. But she seemed to suddenly start having some reservations because she muttered, "Wait." Still, her body definitely told me she wanted me.

Now was not the time for her to be having second thoughts. I kept going. I made it to first base, then slowly kept going, kissing her on the neck first, and after that, working my tongue down over her breasts and toward her navel. I stopped, trying to see if she was gonna force me to go up or if I could go down.

Paisley was lying back on the sofa, her arms around my neck, and I knew she didn't want me to stop. I sucked her navel again, trying to gauge her.

When she spread her legs, I knew I could go anywhere I wanted. I jumped right down to her thighs, kissing the insides like I was trying to strip honey from her flesh. I felt her tremble, and that's when I adjusted her thighs on my shoulders. Next, I nibbled around, sucking and kissing her inner thighs as I slowly stroked her opening.

"Caleb, that feels so good! Please don't stop," she begged.

When I went down farther, she grabbed my head and guided me back to her treasure.

"Oh yes! Right there, right there, baby," she purred.

Trying to give the woman what she wanted, I used one hand to reach up and squeeze her nipple while I sucked her nectar until I felt her juices come down.

When I glanced up, she had a look of satisfaction across her face. "That was real good," she seductively said as she climbed onto my lap.

I eased a condom out of my back pocket and was about to put it on when she took it from me.

"Sit right here in the corner," she instructed as she scooted back and tore the wrapper open with her mouth.

Obediently, I sat down. She eased the condom on me, then climbed back onto my lap, swung one leg over to the side, and slid down on me. The warmth was almost unbearable. She adjusted her hips, wiggling to get it just right.

"Damn, Paisley. Work that on out, girl, work it out," I moaned.

With that, she gyrated even harder, then commenced to ride me until I was ready to explode.

I grabbed her hips, guiding her just so until I felt myself threatening to show her just how good it really was.

I was so turned on, especially when I saw that she was about to come with me.

I squinted my eyes as I endured the pleasurable pain shooting through my body.

After it was over, I fell back, a smile across my face.

"Dang, girl, will you marry me?" I joked.

She pulled herself off me as she smiled herself. "One day, if you're not careful . . ."

I stared at her. Why did it seem like she was serious? But honestly, looking in her eyes at that very moment, I didn't know if that was such a bad thing.

10

Paisley

When I strolled into Houston's Restaurant on Kirby, I spotted Trina's blonde hair (she was trying desperately to emulate Mary J. Blige) right away. She and Brenda were standing near the bar, looking like two hoochies on a mission. Trina had on a spandex baby blue dress with thigh-high boots. Brenda's freshly done braids were cascading down her back and she had on a pair of Apple Bottoms skin-tight jeans and a form-fitting cropped purple halter top.

Trina and Brenda hadn't been seated yet, so the moment I walked in, we followed the hostess to a table tucked in the corner of the dimly lit restaurant.

We settled at the table amid the natural bustling sounds of the place. Just as the hostess walked off, Trina looked at me and started laughing.

"Girl, I don't believe you," she said, shaking her head like she was still trying to wrap her mind around what I had just told her. "I mean, you got him all wrapped up tight and neat, and that's the way it should be done."

"What are you talking about?" I asked. Trina wasn't making any sense.

"The way you snagged Caleb. I mean, you should write a book about how to do it. You know, some women stay on the grind for years and are never able to snag a big dog like Caleb. And so fast." She put her hand up for a high five. "Your ass came, saw, and conquered. Go'n with yo' bad self."

I shook my head, trying not to smile. Since I left her hanging, Brenda reached up and slapped palms with her.

I was trippin' myself. It had been a month and a half since I met Caleb and we talked for hours every day. We had spent every single night together since our first date. I smiled when I thought about that night. We'd had mind-blowing sex. But more than anything, I felt a connection.

It was strange. I knew I probably called Caleb in the first place for all the wrong reasons, but I was spending all my time with him because I was really feeling him.

I knew he'd had an impact on me because I talked about my brother's death and I never talked about my brother to anyone. But there was just something about Caleb that made me open up.

"I can feel you on that one for real, Trina. I'll give you props for her myself," Brenda said, snapping me out of my thoughts.

We turned our heads toward our waitress, who appeared with notepad in hand and a look that read she was in a hurry.

"You ladies ready?"

I quickly rattled off my selection and placed the menu down as I listened to the others do the same. The minute the waitress grabbed all of the menus and scurried away, Trina was back in my face.

"So what does it feel like to have snagged one of Houston's most elusive bachelors?"

I frowned, wondering just when Caleb became an elusive bachelor, when none of us had known a thing about him or his fortune until after the magazine article. Trina was a trip, but I couldn't be mad at her for being herself.

"Girl, I'd be ready to quit my job and prepare for a life of leisure," Trina continued as she leaned back in the chair. "Wait, you don't have a job." She cackled as she gave Brenda another high five.

"Oh, you got jokes," I said. "I do have a job. It may be temporary, but it's a job. And it's something until I can get some more modeling work."

"Well, if you got with Caleb, you wouldn't have to worry about degrading yourself working temporary jobs. And you could spend more time trying to break into the modeling business, and you could do it on somebody else's dime. I'm telling you. Listen to your girl," she said matter-of-factly.

"Umm, there's only one slight problem there, Trina. You ain't had a real job since I've known you. So you don't even know the value of being able to take care of yourself," Brenda joked.

Trina rolled her eyes, then dramatically turned to me. "Like I was saying before, I've worked but it doesn't agree with me. There's nothing wrong with having a man do for you. That, in essence, is taking care of yourself. I know not to waste my time with some lowlife who can't do anything for me. If that's not taking care of myself, I don't know what is," she huffed.

Brenda rolled her eyes and shook her head.

"Either way, girl, I say you should get absolutely everything you can out of him, and get it fast. You never know when next month's flavor is going to pop up and bump you on out the way."

"I know this may sound crazy, but it's not even about the

money anymore. I'm really starting to—" I couldn't finish my thought before she was nearly lunging over the table toward me.

"You're starting to *what*?"

"Dang, let her finish," Brenda interjected.

I contemplated not saying anything, but then thought, if I can't tell my girls, who can I tell? "I think I'm really starting to fall for him," I admitted.

"Oh, that's sweet," Brenda tossed in.

"Sweet, my ass. Oh no, girl, you do *not* want to do that. Don't even get your feelings all bent out of shape by thinking about marriage and a baby carriage. That mess is for the birds! You need to get it while it's available, and get it fast. Men change their minds and their desires quicker than we're able to process it. I'm warning you, love ain't got nothing to do with this. It's cha-ching or buh-bye!" Trina used her hand to wave good-bye. "Besides, you just met this fool. He could be a psycho."

I didn't even feel like fighting this battle so I took my glass of water, enjoyed a sip, and allowed her to go on about how I needed to go for Caleb's wallet instead of his heart. With her neck moving and much attitude flying all over the place, I listened as Trina went on and on about loving the money instead of the man, but little did she know, her advice was already falling on deaf ears.

11

Caleb

"Mama! Dang, will you just listen to what I'm trying to say to you!" I stood in my mother's living room, feeling more like her father than her son. Sometimes the things she did frustrated the hell out of me. And right about now, I was asking myself why I'd even come over here.

"Unh-uh!" she screamed like some ghetto chick. "She wanna act a fool? I'ma show her a fool. She ain't got no business showing up at my house, trying to start some mess!"

I looked toward the dining room, where several place settings were nicely arranged.

My mom had invited Paisley and me over for a birthday lunch for Jenkins, some guy she had hooked up with. They'd been together for a little over a year, but I didn't really care for him. Mama made me promise to give him a chance, so I was here for his party.

I was actually enjoying the evening because Mama and Paisley were really hitting it off. And when I learned that Paisley's mother and my mother had gone to elementary school together, I felt that cinched it—Paisley and I were destined to be together.

We had just sat down for dinner when the doorbell rang.

"Would you like me to get that?" Jenkins asked, getting up from his seat.

I was closest, so I said, "Nah, don't worry about it. I got it."

I made my way to the front door as Mom's best friend, Diane, and her man, as well as Charlene and her husband, continued talking to Paisley.

I opened the door to find a woman standing there with her hands on her hips and her body tilted to one side. She had *attitude* written all over her face. She looked as if she had stepped right off the ghetto bus.

"Good afternoon," I said as I pulled open the door.

"I need to see Marva," she barked.

My mom, who was on her way back into the formal dining room, doubled back and looked toward the front door.

"Who's there, baby?" she asked.

"Ah . . . can I tell her your—?"

"Look, I just need to see Marva, and I need to see her right now!" the woman snapped, all but cutting me off.

Before I could try to calm her down, the other people had stopped and turned their attention to the uninvited visitor.

Mama rushed to my side. "May I help you?" she asked with a look of confusion across her face.

"Yes," the woman answered through an endless stream of tears. She was thin but curvy. A size six if I had to guess. Her long, wavy hair was synthetic, but not the cheap stuff. And although her eyes were red and puffy, her beauty was difficult to hide.

"You're Marva, right?"

I wanted to turn away, but I just had a feeling something wasn't right. I felt that this wasn't the time or the place for whatever this woman had come to say. And my mother certainly didn't need anything ruining all that she was working to create with her friends, none of whom really cared for Jenkins.

That's when he came walking up. "What are you doing here, Paula?"

I closed my eyes and released a breath. I couldn't believe that his voice actually cracked when he said that.

The crying woman cleared her throat and looked at my mother. "Um, well, I hate to tell you this way, but your boyfriend is my baby's daddy. And if you don't believe me, um, well, I brought this birth certificate and picture with me." The woman held out the form and picture as if my mama would want them.

At first, I didn't know quite what to do. The gasps we heard coming from the dining room confirmed that the group had overheard.

"Wait a minute, Marva; hold on just a sec," Jenkins started. My mama looked at the woman, then at Jenkins.

"What is she talking about?" my mother asked.

I rolled my eyes and pulled Mama back. She jerked beyond my reach.

"I'm Paula, and Jenkins moved me here from the East Coast, but now he's found someone else to tickle his fancy, so he thinks he can just toss me to the side like I'm a piece of trash." She wiggled her neck when she talked. I stood there in shock, not believing my fifty-two-year-old mother was caught up in some mess like this.

Jenkins started shifting his weight from one leg to the other as Paula looked me up and down. "Oh, this must be the stepson you talked about. He don't look rich to me," she snapped.

"Why are you at my house?" Mama demanded as she and Jenkins stepped outside. I followed, closing the door behind me so everyone wouldn't witness the drama.

"I just thought you'd want to know about Jenkins, that's all." She wiped away her tears.

"Well, now that I know, get off my property before I call the police and have you thrown in jail for trespassing."

She turned to Jenkins. He said, "Wait, Marva, I don't know what she's talking about."

"If it ain't true, then why was you with me just last night? You told me she was having this fancy party for you. How would I know that if it wasn't true? You said you were just using her for her money!" Paula snapped. "How would I know her son makes all this money if you didn't tell me?"

"Marva, I'll be back, baby. Let me deal with this." He grabbed Paula by the arm and dragged her toward her car, obviously trying to shut her up.

I looked at my mother. Her bottom lip was trembling. I knew she was probably more embarrassed than anything else.

"He ain't even worth it, Mama," I said, moving closer to her.

She looked up at me, her eyes pooling. "Why do I have such bad luck with men?"

"It's not you, Mama, it's them; trust me, it's not you," I consoled. She collapsed onto my chest and started sobbing. I stood there, rubbing her back and fighting the urge to go put my foot up Jenkins's ass. Then I thought back to years of watching my mama stumble through this love mess.

I recall one night something woke me out of my sleep. I got up from my bed and quietly walked toward the door, then pressed my ear against it, listening to hear if Mama and Roger were in the midst of another fight. He hadn't been around for a couple of weeks, and Mama swore about all the things she'd do to him the moment he showed his face.

I was fifteen at the time. I crept out of my bedroom to find my mother rummaging through drawers in the kitchen.

"What you lookin' for?" I asked, rubbing sleep from my eyes. She jumped, her Afro nearly touching the light fixture above.

"Boy, what you doin' up? Go on back to bed now!" she snapped.

I stood there looking at her because something just didn't seem right.

"Um, I was gonna leave you a note," she said, her eyes searching the room but never looking directly at me.

"A note?"

"Yeah, um, Roger called and he wants me to meet him at the bus station," she said nervously.

I scratched my head, trying to make sense of what she was saying. My mom had been through her share of men. My dad had abandoned her when she was six months' pregnant; I had only ever met him one time. She was married to Damon's dad long enough to conceive him, but he moved on and wasn't in Damon's life either. She went from man to man, each time talking about how she was sure this one was "the one."

"I thought you were mad at Roger," I said.

"That was before I talked to him and he sent me a ticket. He needs me to meet him in Waco," she said.

"Cool, what about school?" I asked, getting excited, thinking I'd finally get out of classes for a few weeks.

"Um, he only sent one ticket," she said softly.

For some reason, I still didn't get what she was saying. "I'll go get my stuff," I said, turning to go to my room. "And I'll wake up Damon."

"Caleb, you all aren't going, not this time. Mama just needs a little break, but I'll be back," she said, moving toward me. I moved to try to get out of her way.

"Huh?" She wasn't making sense. That's when I noticed the old, tattered suitcase by the door.

"So, you were just gonna leave, without even saying anything?" I asked.

"It's not like that. I was gonna call," she defended.

"Mama, this is crazy. You just gon' up and leave us?" I was mad, but more than anything, I couldn't imagine what she planned to do about us. "Who's gon' watch us?"

"Boy, you damn near grown, now. You can watch your brother." She stared at me, looking like she was fighting off tears. "I need you to be a man. I'll be back, now you just go on back to bed and I'll return before you know it."

This wasn't making any sense to me. How could she possibly expect me to take care of myself, let alone my brother?

I wanted to protest some more, but I think I was just too stunned.

"I left y'all a couple of dollars," she said, pointing to the counter.

"When are you coming back?" I was struggling not to cry like some little baby. I was trying to "man up," but the pain in my heart was stiff.

"I'll be back when I get back. Just know that I love you. Both of you. Make sure Damon knows that. I just gotta get away."

My mother leaned in and kissed my cheek. I had so many things I wanted to say, but no words would come out. I just watched in disbelief as she walked out of the house.

That was the hardest time of my life. Damon had been devastated and stayed mad all the time, and the little money my mother left ran out after one trip to the grocery store. Each day that passed caused me to grow more and more bitter.

My mother did come back, a month later. But it might as well have been five years later, because I thought I was going to lose my mind.

I was glad to see her, but I never looked at her the same again. For a long time, whenever she walked out the door, I wondered if she was running off with some man.

Over the years, we'd grown closer, and I'd even forgiven her. But that betrayal—that was something I'd never forget.

Now, standing here holding my mother, I couldn't help but wonder if my attraction to these drama queens had anything to do with what I've witnessed my mama go through. Mom had spent her life searching for love in all the wrong places. I had hoped by buying her this nice house, retiring her, and giving her a worry-free lifestyle, things would finally get better for her. I was about to tell her as much when Jenkins walked over to my mother.

"Marva, can I talk to you, baby?" he said, ignoring my glare.

I just knew my mother would tell him where he could go, especially since her friends were all peeking out the window. But my mother sniffed again, then nodded as she motioned for Jenkins to walk on the side of the house.

I couldn't believe it. I told myself to just give her a minute. No doubt she was out there telling him where he could go. I went back inside to wait. Fifteen minutes later, she walked back in the kitchen, where I'd been pacing back and forth.

"Caleb, I know I got a little upset, but everything's fine," she softly said.

I looked at her, at him, then back at her again. "Mama, are you for real? You don't need that fool. You're living nice, you don't have to worry about anything. Forget about him."

She took a deep breath as Jenkins walked up behind her and put his arm around her waist. "Caleb, I know you don't understand." She wiped her eyes. "I'm thankful for all you've done for me, but none of this means nothing if you don't have someone who truly loves you to share it with." She looked at me with pity. "One day you'll get that."

With that, she took Jenkins's hand and led him back into the dining room with her friends as if nothing had ever happened.

12

Caleb

I had to admit, Paisley had done good. I mean, a picnic in the middle of the day. At first I wasn't feeling it when she suggested that we spend our lunch break under the trees at Transco Tower. I think I was still in a foul mood from my mother and that drama from yesterday.

But Paisley had sold me on the picnic in the park thing, and honestly it was turning out quite nice.

We were sitting under a towering tree with branches that draped over the spot where Paisley had laid out a blanket. I had just finished reading a chapter of HoneyB's freaky book *Sexcapades*. I think having me read to her turned her on because she kept squirming and looking at me all seductively.

"You want any more wine?" she asked as she held up the bottle.

"Naw. I do have to get back to work, you know."

She smiled that beautiful smile that was stealing my heart.

"I guess I need to lay off too"—she laughed lightly—"because this wine has me wanting to open my heart. I don't need to be drinking in the middle of the day anyway."

I brushed a loose curl from her face. "I want you to open your heart."

She playfully pushed me back. "Naw, you ain't ready for what I'm feeling."

"I'm past ready," I replied, "'cause I'm feeling it too."

We stared at each other for a minute, then our lips slowly met. As our tongues played tag, I couldn't help but think how what I was feeling went so much deeper than lusting after a fine woman.

We finally pulled apart. "I love you Caleb. I know it may be crazy because stuff is just moving so fast, but I do."

I stared into her eyes. "I love you too. And I don't want to figure out the hows, the whys, or question whether it's moving too fast. I just want to enjoy what I'm feeling for you."

She smiled as we leaned in and kissed again.

After releasing her from my embrace, I looked at my watch and was just about to tell her I needed to be heading back when I noticed the stunned expression on her face as she stared straight ahead.

Turning to see what she was looking at, I noticed a tall, muscular man standing only a few feet away, cracking his knuckles. When he saw me looking, he nodded his head, turned, and walked off.

"Who was that?"

Paisley started gathering up the things. "Nobody."

I looked at her, then at the man who was stomping away. "That doesn't look like nobody to me."

"Just drop it, Caleb. Please."

My mood was suddenly shifting. She must have me confused. "No, I'm not gon' be able to do that." With that, I stood up. "I'll ask again. Who was that?" That Negro had looked psychotic.

She stood up too. "Can we just go?"

"Paisley, is that your man or something?"

She shook her head. "I told you, I don't have a boyfriend. I wouldn't be sitting out here talking about how much I love you if I had a boyfriend."

"Then who was that?"

"That was my coworker who has a crush on me."

"Why is he acting like he's mad at you?"

"He's just a trip."

"How did he know you were here?"

Paisley shrugged. "He heard me on the phone inviting you to lunch. His cubicle is next to mine."

I felt myself getting pissed because homeboy was straight disrespecting me.

"I've filed a sexual harassment complaint against him, but because I'm temporary, I really don't think they are taking it seriously. Besides, my supervisor says they really can't do anything until the investigation is complete," Paisley said.

I looked over and noticed the guy standing against the side of the building, staring at us, a crazed look across his face.

"What's his name? He looks crazy."

"Dirk."

"What the hell kind of name is Dirk?"

She shrugged. "He's only crazy when he can't have what he wants."

"And I take it he wants you?"

She nodded.

Dirk blew her a kiss, shot me an evil look, then turned around and walked to his car.

I felt my heart racing. I was ready to hurt somebody. "Hell, naw. This ain't gon' fly. You need to quit that job."

She looked at me as if I were a special ed student doing Chinese arithmetic. "Quit my job? I'm trying to save up money to get a new portfolio together, not to mention all of my bills."

"You said you hated that job anyway. Plus, you said it yourself, you're just temporary."

"Yeah, temporary until the girl comes off medical leave, which could be another three months."

"You need to be pursuing something you really like—like modeling."

Paisley blew an exasperated breath. "What part of it takes money to model do you not get? And my bills, hello?"

"Money isn't an issue," I replied.

"For you, maybe." She threw her purse over her shoulder and turned to head back toward her office.

I took her hand and turned her toward me to get her to see that I was serious. "Look, I wouldn't ask you to quit your job if I didn't plan to take care of you."

"Caleb, what are you saying?"

"How much do you make there?"

"I don't make a lot, but it's enough to pay my bills."

"How much?" I repeated.

She looked unsure about sharing her information with me. Finally she sighed. "I make about twenty-five hundred a month."

I pulled out my checkbook and quickly made out a check. "Here."

She took it and looked at it. "That's three thousand dollars."

"That's enough to get you by this month. I'll give you the same thing next month and every month after that until you find another job, preferably a modeling gig."

Paisley stared at the check, then handed it back to me. "I can't ask you to do this."

I pushed her hand away. "You didn't ask me. I don't want my woman working with some psycho stalker."

"Oh, I'm your woman now." She smiled. "Just because of what I said?"

"I said it too, remember?" I pulled her to me and wrapped my arms around her waist. "So you damn straight you're my woman. And my woman will not be working with some psycho stalker like Dirk."

Paisley looked like she wanted to protest some more, but then she looked down at the check. "Are you sure about this?"

"I've never been more sure."

"But, Caleb, I mean, we haven't even known each other that long. This may be a bit too much." She tried to hand the check back to me again.

I put my hands up in the air, refusing to take it. "Tell me you really don't want that money."

She smiled. "Of course I'd like to take it. I just can't."

"You can." I pushed her hand back. "And you will. It's just money. What's the big deal?"

"Spoken like someone with money," she mumbled as she shook her head.

I lifted her chin and our eyes met. "Paisley, I look forward to loving you and this is just a small way for me to show you that. That's just how I operate. I'm a love-at-first-sight kind of guy. And I knew you were a woman I could love the first time I laid eyes on you."

She blushed. "You were in *lust* at first sight."

"Okay, you may be right about that, because you are fine as hell." I grinned. "But I know now I want more than your body." I pulled her to me again. "I want your heart."

As I stared at Paisley, I couldn't help but think that she offered it all: beauty, brains, intelligence. I'd finally met my soul mate and I couldn't have been happier.

13

Caleb

Todd stood in the doorway of my condo, shaking his head. "Man, your ass goes from one extreme to the other," he said.

"What?"

"You're really gon' move this girl you've known less than two months in with you? It's bad enough you had her quit her job after knowing her a month, but now, you've convinced her to give up her crib and move in here with you?"

I set down the box I was carrying. "Todd, we've been through this a hundred times. Her rent was past due and when she went to pay it, the landlord said it was too late. He'd already rented out her place. So she didn't have a choice and it just didn't make sense for her to go get another apartment."

"And why not?"

I was tired of going around and around with Todd. "Man, I told you. It's just something about her. She's the one."

"That's the same thing you said about Asia. And every other woman you've been with."

I wasn't going to let him spoil my good mood. I was actually excited to have Paisley move in with me. She'd been against the idea at first and had even planned to move back to Fifth Ward with her mother, in an old home I'd never seen but that Paisley had said was extremely dilapidated. "I love her," I said. "I can't help it. Can't control how long it's been. I just know that I love her." I pushed him to the side as I slid the box against the wall.

"All I'm sayin' is you need to slow your roll, bruh."

"Whatever. This time is for real. Can you believe our mothers went to elementary school together? That's divine, man."

Todd stared blankly at me before pulling out his cell phone and putting it to his ear. "Hello?" He handed the phone to me. "It's the psychic Miss Cleo. She said to tell you that's some *divine* bullshit."

I moved another box up against the dining room wall.

"And how much stuff does this girl have?" He walked over to a box labeled PERSONAL ITEMS, reached in, and pulled out a string with small balls on it. "Is this what I think it is?"

I snatched it from him. "Man, get out of her stuff."

"Damn. At least she's a freak."

"You need to chill out."

"Oh, here we go with this, 'Don't talk about Paisley; she's my girl,'" he mimicked.

"You're the one that told me to get a dime. Is she not a dime?" I motioned toward the bar where I had an eight-by-ten photo of her.

Todd fingered the photo. "That she is. Good God Almighty." He shook out of his trance. "Yeah, I told you to get a dime. That didn't mean move her in with you."

"The heart wants what it wants."

"Here we go with this." Todd laughed. "Man, why do you do this?"

"Do what?"

Todd's tone turned serious. "Jump into these relationships so fast, give your heart so freely. I mean, is this about your mom?"

I cut my eyes at him. I couldn't believe he went there. He knew I didn't like talking about the situation with my mother.

Todd must've known he was about to tread into territory he didn't have any business treading. He threw his hands up. "You know what? Forget I said anything. You wanna move this chick in, move her in." He took a swig of his water bottle.

"I wanna move her in," I replied, a stern look across my face.

"I guess if you gon' pay for her, might as well have her under your roof," he mumbled.

"What is that supposed to mean?" I snapped.

"Nothing, man, nothing at all," Todd replied as he watched Paisley walk in. She was all smiles as she directed the movers upstairs with some of her stuff.

"How much stuff is she moving in?" he quietly asked.

I threw him a look to let him know to chill. The last thing I wanted was for Paisley to be trippin' with him.

A few minutes later, she came bouncing back down the stairs.

"Hey, Todd," she said.

I'd introduced them last week and was glad that they actually seemed to click. But of course, that was before I broke the news that she was moving in with me.

"What's up, Paisley? I see you're getting settled," Todd said.

I took a deep breath, hoping he wouldn't start any mess.

Paisley draped her arm through mine. "Yes. Everything is just moving so fast, but I couldn't be happier."

"I bet you couldn't," he mumbled sarcastically. Luckily, Paisley didn't hear him because she had turned her attention back to the movers. She seemed on cloud nine as she moved her stuff in. But my happiness seemed to be fading because of the look on Todd's face, the one that seemed to say I was doing it again—setting myself up to be gotten by a gold digger.

14

Caleb

I was so happy to see Paisley and my friends hitting it off. Actually they were doing more than that, they were having a really good time. We all were.

Paisley and I were at dinner at La Strada with Todd and his freak of the week; my brother, Damon, and his date; and Dedra and her boyfriend, Marcus.

It was Paisley's birthday and while she was going out with her friends tomorrow night, I wanted to celebrate and I thought, what better time for everyone to get to know her. I'd reserved the wine room and the evening had been going great from the moment we all came together.

Paisley fit right in with her sparkling smile and winning personality. She'd even broken down Damon's wall, and right now he was sitting over there giggling like he'd known and liked her for years.

I smiled, just another reason why I loved that girl. I had taken her to an event for my job last week and she fit right in, dazzling those white boys like it was nothing.

Todd, Damon, and even Dedra had been tripping over how quickly our relationship was moving along, but neither of us could help how we felt.

"Okay, Caleb, she gets a passing grade from me," Damon professed as Paisley leaned in and squeezed his arm. "She likes the rapper Common and thinks 50 Cent is overrated. That's my kind of girl."

I took her hand. "Good. Now that that's settled, I guess that means I can marry her then." I was joking, but silence covered the room and every eye at the table turned to me, including Paisley's.

Damon's smile immediately left his face. "Marry?"

Even Paisley couldn't mask the stunned expression on her face.

"I—I was just messing around," I said. But then I thought about it. "But, yeah"—I rubbed her back—"I'd love to marry Paisley," I said, gazing into her beautiful eyes.

"You can't be serious," Dedra said. Out of the corner of my eye, I could see her shaking her head in disbelief.

Paisley shot Dedra a warning look.

"Ah . . . I didn't mean it like that," Dedra stuttered. "It's just . . . well, let's face it, you two barely even know each other."

Marcus took Dedra's hand. "I don't know. I think it's kinda sweet." He shrugged.

Dedra quickly snatched her hand from him. "There's nothing sweet about rushing into marriage," she said adamantly.

Paisley ignored her and turned her attention back to me. "Well, I think it's sweet too. You can know a person for years and still not know who they truly are. Besides, I'm sure Caleb's not talking about getting married right now."

I didn't know what she meant by that. "Oh, so you wouldn't marry me now?" I questioned.

"Do you want me to marry you now?" she challenged.

I noticed the glances I was catching from Todd and Damon, but I ignored them both.

"I think we should do it. I mean, think about it. How long does it take to really get to know a person? I've heard that some of the longest-lasting marriages are those where people either hadn't been together long or the marriages were arranged."

"Yeah, but in this day and age, nobody in their right mind would do something like that." Dedra chuckled and then glanced around the room. No one else said a word.

I looked at Todd, who still hadn't said a word and was just sitting there with a stunned look on his face.

"Girl, don't be no fool," Todd's date said. "Marriage is overrated."

Both Paisley and I turned our noses up at her. I know I didn't mean to be rude, but nobody even knew this chick's name. We definitely weren't trying to listen to her two cents.

"So, well, what do you say, Paisley?" I asked, trying to shake the nervousness from my voice.

"What does she say about *what*?" Todd finally said.

"Yeah, dawg, I mean, what are you doing, man?" Damon said.

"Sounds to me like he's proposing," Marcus said, his voice laced with a hint of jealousy.

My eyes were focused on Paisley's and hers on mine. I noticed the corners of her lips curling into what looked like a nervous smile. I think I even noticed her trembling a little. I took her hands into mine, hoping to calm her a bit.

"We could spend the rest of our lives getting to know each other, loving each other, and just being there for one another, getting old together," I offered.

Her eyes began to pool.

"Awww, is this the sweetest thing or what," Todd's girl sang. "But still, girl, don't do it."

Everyone ignored her.

"I want you to be my wife," I said softly.

"Are you serious?" Paisley asked in a voice that I had never heard her use before.

I nodded. The curl of her lips turned into a full-blown smile.

"Caleb, man, what's going on here?" Damon asked as if he were on trial for a crime he didn't commit.

I ignored him too.

"Do you love me?" I asked her. Suddenly it was as if we were in the room alone. No one else mattered as far as I was concerned. A few teardrops escaped Paisley's eyes.

"You can't be serious," I heard Dedra say.

"Let that man do his thang," Marcus warned.

"I love you so much," Paisley cried with trembling lips.

"Then make me a happy man; say you'll marry me, Paisley," I urged. "I don't have a ring because this is unexpected. But I'm speaking from the heart, baby. We can go get your rock first thing in the morning."

The tears streamed faster as she vigorously nodded her head, saying, "Yes! Yes! I'll be your wife, Caleb. I'll marry you!"

I quickly stood and scooped her into my arms. We shared a kiss, not the kind where lips touch in a quick peck. But this one was tongues dancing and lips smacking against each other, one that told the rest of our party that nothing they did or said mattered.

When we separated, Paisley used her fingers to dab at the corners of her mouth and eyes as she giggled. I was thrilled, that is, until I looked around the room and again confirmed that no one else seemed to be sharing in our joy.

Dedra sat with her arms folded across her chest.

"So y'all getting hitched for real?" Damon asked, like he hadn't just witnessed the proposal.

Todd was far too busy shaking his head to even comment, but the look on his face spoke volumes. Without words, he told me he thought I was making the biggest mistake of my life.

I acknowledged his concern with a slight nod and a silent vow to prove him and all of the other naysayers dead wrong.

When Todd finally spoke, I sat back, wishing he hadn't.

"I guess it's all good, man," he said, still nodding his head. "I mean, y'all really don't know a thing about each other. You haven't even been together long enough to have an argument." He shrugged. "But hey, that's what they make prenups for."

"Amen to that!" Damon casually tossed in.

"Prenups?" Todd's girl asked, her face all scrunched up.

"Yeah, of course my boy is making her sign a prenup. It's a way to cover his ass . . . ets."

"Todd, you're talking crazy," Paisley finally said.

"What's so crazy about it?" I asked. Her head snapped in my direction. "I mean, I love you and all, but I ain't stupid," I declared.

She eased her body away from mine, frowned, and looked at me. "What exactly is that supposed to mean?"

"Let's face it, Paisley; I'm worth a considerable amount of money. Todd is right. It would be foolish for me to make such a rash decision without taking the proper steps to protect my interests."

"Fo' real!" Damon said, like I had finally come to my senses.

"You know what? This isn't even the right time or place to discuss this," Paisley said, throwing up her hands.

"Why not?" Dedra wanted to know.

She and Paisley had a staring match, but no one said another word.

"Dawg, just handle your business," Todd warned. "That's all I'm saying."

Finally, Paisley turned away from Dedra and said, "His business is mine, and mine is his."

"I know that's right. Girl, get yours," Todd's date said.

"Who the hell are you again?" Damon asked, rolling his eyes.

She grabbed a drink and leaned back in her chair. "I'm Paisley's conscience." She smirked.

"This ain't about business anyway," Dedra added, her brow furrowing. "It's about Caleb being careful."

"Look here, Miss Secretary," Paisley said, leaning in. "Why don't you just take care of writing the memos and let me and my fiancé handle our money."

"*Our?* Don't look like to me you got none," Dedra snapped.

Paisley was getting heated. "Don't worry about what I got. I got Caleb, and that's all that matters!"

It was past time for me to step in. "C'mon, you two. Let's not ruin the night with all this kind of talk. I agree with Paisley; we can talk about this later." I started looking around the room. "I need to get some champagne up in here. What kind of celebration is this with no bubbly?"

I motioned for the waiter and asked that he bring us another bottle of champagne. But I could tell from the look on everyone's faces—the party was definitely over.

15

Paisley

This sitting at home all day was about to drive me insane. Trina might enjoy being a kept woman, but me, I had issues with just sitting around, waiting on a man to give me money.

But that's just what I'd been doing for the past two weeks. At first, it was cute and all. I mean, we'd kinda let the whole prenup thing die, thankfully. And I was now living the life my mom always dreamed about. I finally had love *and* money. Even still, I felt that I was put on this earth to do more than just sit around and eat bonbons all day.

I'd actually been out job hunting, but Caleb was right, the whole sitting behind a desk all day wasn't for me. I was trying to find modeling work, but so far I hadn't had any luck.

Of course, Caleb tried to reassure me, and I did like having money in my account. Shoot, the people at the bank were probably trying to figure out what was going on since I hadn't bounced a check since I'd met Caleb.

The phone rang, startling me out of my thoughts. I assumed it was Caleb, who called me twenty times a day just to see what I was doing. He was in Los Angeles, meeting with two potential clients, and wouldn't be back for three days.

I smiled when I saw Trina's number on the caller ID.

"What's up, diva?" she sang.

"Nothing. Absolutely nothing," I replied.

"Shoot, that's the life. To have nothing up and all your bills paid. You can't beat that shit."

"Whatever." I shook my head. Trina worked only part-time at a travel agency, but you'd have sworn she worked out in some cornfield or something.

"Okay, back up. You want to tell me why you sounding like somebody killed your cat? Girl, you've snagged a gold mine."

"This lying around all day watching soap operas is getting old. I need to find a job, any job, until something breaks open in modeling."

"What? Getting paid can never get old."

"Yeah, it really can." I leaned back and propped my feet up on Caleb's Paladin coffee table. He would have a heart attack if he walked in and saw me with my feet on the table.

"I don't know. It's just something about knowing that any minute Caleb can decide he doesn't want to give me another dime, and I'm out on the streets. I don't like that."

"That's why whatever he gives you, you put up half and blow the other half. And always tell him what he's giving you isn't enough, so you need more. Shoot, you milk that cow until it runs dry."

Why was I trying to reason with the queen gold digger?

"Ooooh, Lord, have mercy," Trina said. "Speaking of cash cows, a fine-ass brother with a briefcase, a BlackBerry, and a two-thousand-dollar suit just passed by. Gotta go." Trina slammed down the phone before I could say another word.

I shook my head at my crazy friend, then picked up the remote and began flipping through the channels. I stopped on *The Maury Povich Show.* After watching some woman say she was 150 percent sure her boyfriend was her son's father—which, by the way, he wasn't—I'd had enough. I had to get out of the house.

I changed into my I AM Fashions sweat suit and made my way downstairs, figuring I'd go do a little shopping.

When I finally arrived downstairs and walked toward my car, I noticed a chauffeur standing next to a limo. The only reason I even looked was because I felt him looking at me.

"Are you Paisley Terrell?"

"It depends on who wants to know," I said, my curiosity building. I immediately started looking around to make sure possible witnesses were on hand in case anything went down.

"I am here on behalf of Bobby Trumane. He'd like you to meet him at the airport. Don't worry about packing anything. He'll buy everything you need once you get to your destination." The clean-cut man looked at his watch before opening the door.

"I'm not about to just hop in a limo with someone I don't know." My brows twitched up in disbelief. I didn't add that I wasn't going anywhere with Bobby, of all people. Although I'm not gon' lie, the whole 007 stuff was piquing my interest, especially because I had always told Bobby I would love for a man to just come and whisk me away somewhere. *Now* he decided to listen.

"I thought you'd say that."

I leaned in toward the limo and almost died when Bobby stepped out. He looked so damn good, it was unbelievable. He was wearing a tailored golden-brown Armani suit. His fade was freshly faded, and his skin looked like silk. In fact, he looked like he had just stepped off the pages of *GQ* magazine. It had been only a few months, but this was not the same man I had busted on national TV.

"Let's talk," he said before I could even say hello.

"About what?" I crossed my arms to let him know I wasn't falling for his game, no matter how good he was looking. "And how did you find me?"

"Number one, I just listened for your heart. It led me straight to you."

I groaned at that corny line.

"Number two," he continued, "I wanted to surprise you with a trip so we can at least talk about a few things. I bet you didn't realize that time-share we bought in Jamaica two years ago was about to expire. We'll lose the money we pumped into it on the thirty-first. And what do you know? That's next week."

I had forgotten all about that. I definitely didn't need to be losing my money.

"Besides, I've got the airfare covered. You won't have to spend a dime."

I guess Bobby could tell I was thinking about it because he said, "Why don't you at least ride with me to the airport; then if you decide you don't want to go, I'll understand."

"Where did you get the money for all of this?" I motioned toward the limo.

"I know you always thought I was dreaming big, baby. But I knew I could do it. I signed not one but two NBA clients, including Kyle Morris."

"The high school superstar who went first in the draft?"

"The one and only. And everything he gets, I get fifteen percent."

Damn, I thought. *Why couldn't he have hit a lick like that when we were together?*

"Come on, Paisley." Bobby stepped closer to me. "You stood by me when I was flat broke. Let me repay you. Plus, remember, you don't want to lose your money on the time-share." A huge smile crossed his face.

I tried to ignore his smile, but the more I thought about what he was saying, the more I asked myself, did I want to take a chance and mess up things with Caleb?

"No strings attached, none whatsoever, I swear. Just you, me, a beach with crystal clear blue water, sunshine, and relaxation." He held up his ticket.

I couldn't believe I was standing outside my boyfriend's condo contemplating whether I should take a free weekend getaway with my ex.

"I just don't know," I said.

"What are you unsure about? You need your own room? It's done. I just want us together, that's all I want. We go have a great weekend, come back, you go your way, I go mine, if that's what you want. It's that simple." He shrugged as if he were offering me a piece of cheesecake instead of a trip that could lead to a passionate encounter.

"Bobby, I'm engaged." I held out the three-carat rock Caleb and I had picked out the day after he proposed.

"Umpphh . . . he couldn't do no better than that?"

I jerked my hand back and rolled my eyes.

Bobby stepped toward me. "Paisley, do you still have feelings for me?"

"I am so over you, Bobby." I said it although I damn sure didn't believe it. Why the hell was my stomach turning backflips? This fool had cheated on me.

"Prove it."

"I don't have to prove a thing."

"Before you marry this dude—whoever he is—shouldn't you make sure I'm out of your system?" Bobby said with a smirk. "We don't have to do a thing. Honestly, I just want to do something nice for you—for us—for you. I owe you that m-m-much." He stuttered as he raised his hands in surrender. "I swear, we won't do a thing. We don't have to. I'll get you your own room, I promise," he begged.

He had to have known he was breaking me. I wanted to go, but I didn't want him to think this was a path back to my heart again. I was with Caleb now and didn't want Bobby to get any ideas. But I couldn't help it, I was curious *and* excited.

Bobby shrugged and flashed that beautiful smile again.

"Nothing is going to happen!" I warned.

"Scout's honor," he promised.

"But I need . . ." I looked toward the condo.

"We can buy whatever you need. We'll get everything once we arrive there."

I took a deep breath. Caleb was going to blow a gasket. "Okay, but I mean it when I say nothing is going to happen." I tried to make that very, very clear.

The thought of spending time alone with him in a romantic setting wasn't high on my list, but I was so excited about the prospect of a spur-of-the-moment trip. And I didn't want to waste my money, after all.

"I can't believe I'm whisking off to fun in the sun, like it ain't nothing," I mumbled as I stood and waited for him to motion me into the limo.

"You will be happy you did."

"Wait a minute," I said. I couldn't just totally disappear. I ran upstairs, quickly grabbed a few things, and left Caleb a note, just in case he came back early. He was going to have a fit, but I would just have to deal with him when I got back. Hopefully, I would get back before him anyway.

As we headed to the airport, I tried to call Trina to let her know where I was going, but then thought she'd just try to use this as a way to prove her point that money mattered more than the heart. Forget it. I snapped my phone closed and enjoyed the ride.

16

Caleb

I couldn't even begin to tell you what Jerroll Hunt was talking about. I was supposed to be here wooing him, convincing him to sign with our company, but my mind was so clouded I couldn't even concentrate. My first meeting with another client yesterday had gone well, but today was a whole different story.

"Dude, what's up?" Jerroll asked. We were sitting in the bar area of Los Angeles's exclusive W Hotel. The area was bustling with after-fivers and it was the place I usually came to close important deals.

I debated whether I should tell him the truth—that I was pissed off because I couldn't get in touch with my girl. I'd tried calling her all day, and she wasn't answering her cell or my text messages. I'd even called her mother. First she told me Paisley wasn't there. Then she tried to cover it up, like she was on her way over there. I could tell she was lying and that was making me even more suspicious.

But it was the last call to Paisley, right before I came into this meeting with Jerroll, that had my nerves working overtime. The phone had rung once, then didn't ring again. She'd sent me back a text that read, *Can't talk now. Just trust that I love you. We'll talk on Monday.*

Monday? It was Friday.

"Man, I'm sorry. I just got some stuff weighing on my mind," I replied.

Jerroll took a sip of his drink. "Women things, huh?"

I tried to laugh. "That obvious?"

Jerroll nodded. "Look, why don't you go on and handle your business. There's no need to sell me on your company. I'm sold. Have your attorneys send my agent the paperwork and we'll take it from there."

"Are you sure?" I hated being unprofessional, but my mind was not focusing; I couldn't even think straight.

"Yeah, man. Go handle your business."

I breathed a sigh of relief as I took some money out of my pocket and threw it on the table. "Thanks, Jerroll. I really appreciate this."

Without another word, I raced up to my room, tossed my stuff in my suitcase, and headed outside to catch a cab. After giving the cabdriver an extra twenty to get me to the airport ASAP, I dialed Paisley's number again and, of course, got her voice mail. Now it was going straight to the voice mail, like she'd cut the phone off.

I looked at the text message again as the cab arrived. *Can't talk now. Just trust that I love you. We'll talk on Monday.*

What the hell did that mean?

I leaned back in the cab. I couldn't focus as I continued to try to analyze the e-mail.

Three months. Why am I going through all of this for a girl I've known only three months? The voices were dancing in my head. *This couldn't be healthy. I need to move on. I need to just trust that nothing's wrong. I need for Paisley to answer the phone.*

I got to the airport and boarded the next flight out. Right after takeoff I fell asleep.

I don't know how long I'd been asleep, I just know I popped up in a sweat when the stewardess woke me, asking me to raise my seat back.

It took me a minute to register where I was. I wiped my forehead, beaded with sweat, just as my dream started coming back to me. In it, Paisley was walking down the aisle of a massive church. I was waiting for her at the altar. But before she reached me, she turned to some man in the audience and smiled. He stood and said, "Don't do it, Paisley. Come with me. I can give you a much better life."

She looked at me and instead of walking toward me, she turned and went to him, muttering, "I'm sorry, Caleb. He's richer than you."

Then I turned to my mother in tears, but instead of embracing me, she too had said, "Sorry, baby, I gotta go. Jenkins wants me to run away with him."

I looked up and the entire church was empty. Everyone had left me.

I shook my head, trying to get my bearings back. "Man, that was crazy," I muttered. "What was that about?"

I was just about to try to analyze it when I realized where I was headed. No, that's what I needed to be focused on. Where was my woman? That's what I needed to be thinking about. I didn't need to be thinking about some crazy dream.

I felt a sense of relief when the plane finally touched down. I think I was probably the first one off. I didn't mean to be rude as I almost ran over people, but I was on a mission. I had to find my girl so she could tell me that the crazy thoughts swirling in my head were all just in my imagination.

17

Caleb

"Paisley must be out of her mind," I snarled as I eased back in the chair and tried, to no avail, to get comfortable. The truth was, there was really no way to get comfortable while waiting in the dark for your woman to come home after she's been missing in action for the past three days. I just sat staring at the digital clock on the entertainment console.

"I don't know who the hell she thinks I am, but I ain't the one." I rubbed my face and sighed.

I was hopeful at first when this waiting game started. Quite surely she'd be coming home any moment now—that's what I told myself when it started. But the digital clock had long ago confirmed that it was four-fifteen in the morning. Four-fifteen in the morning and Paisley's ass was nowhere to be found.

I didn't trip too much when I first got home late Friday night, thinking, okay, she's out with Trina. She's not expecting me back until Monday, so maybe she's just hanging with Trina. Of course, Trina wasn't answering her phone, so I had no way of knowing for sure.

Then Saturday and Sunday I tried to bury myself in my work. But now, here it was Monday morning, and I ain't heard a peep outta her. To say I was pissed didn't even begin to describe how I was feeling right then.

A part of me didn't even want her ass to come back. I mean, really, where in the hell could she be but with another man?

I had hoped she would come home before now. I figured a couple of nights out, we could fix it. But when Saturday night crept into Sunday morning, then so on, I finally decided not to call her cell anymore. I mean, let's face it. After what, a hundred or so unanswered calls, it was obvious she didn't want to be bothered with me.

By the time I gave up on the phone calls, I had moved from the living room to the den to the bedroom and back to the living room. Now I was sitting at the kitchen table, mad as hell. If she walked in this moment, she wouldn't be able to see me. I wanted this vantage point just to see how she'd try to work this lie out.

When I noticed the clock blaring five-thirty, I told myself to go to bed. I was just about to get up when I heard keys jingling at the door. Suddenly I became alert and caught a burst of energy. I listened intently as she fumbled with the keys. Cautiously I stood and moved closer to the wall, hoping to avoid being detected. My car was parked in the back, my way of lulling her into a false sense of comfort.

She eased in through the door and looked up toward our bedroom. The moonlight was highlighting the stress on her face as she hesitated, then slipped her bags onto the floor. It was obvious she was returning from some sort of trip. I wondered what she was thinking, if she was even thinking at all.

Instead of going upstairs, she sat on the sofa and buried her face in her palms. I could see her shoulders moving slightly up and down like she was sobbing. I figured she must've done some interesting things on that trip to make her so damn emotional.

I eased into the living room and leaned against the door. "Ain't no use in crying about it now."

She jumped at the sound of my voice and looked at me through wide but red eyes. Her mouth was agape.

"Don't even bother." I walked over and switched on the light as I glanced at her bags, then back at her.

"Caleb, I'm so sorry," she started.

"Nah, you ain't sorry. Wait, I take that back. You *are* sorry. You think I'm some kind of fool or something?" My intention had been to let her try to explain, but when she opened her mouth, I just lost it.

She jumped up from the sofa and rushed to put her arms around my neck. I tried to pull away and she just clung tighter.

"Get the hell off me, Paisley!" I managed to push her away from me.

"Just hear me out," she said, tears trickling down her cheeks. "Nothing happened—I swear! Why do you think I'm back here now?"

"Maybe because whoever you been with is done with your ass! Of course you're gonna come back here now. Where else are you gonna go?"

She buried her face in her hands again and sobbed louder this time.

"Cut the drama. Your ass wasn't thinking about crying while I was sitting here worrying about you, were you?" I was so mad, I could have wrung her neck with my bare hands. "Don't try to play me, Paisley. At least show me that much respect. Hey, you made your choice, plain and simple. When you decided not to bring your ass home, or even call for that matter, you made your choice."

"But it's not what you think," she cried, looking up at me. "Bobby just—"

"*Bobby?* You were with your ex, Bobby?" I laughed. "Ain't this a bitch?" I turned my back and walked away. I had to leave before I lost my damn mind and hurt somebody. As I made my way up the stairs, I could hear her crying even louder. But I didn't care. I went into our bedroom, pulled the closet open, and started yanking her stuff from the hangers. I stuffed everything into large trash bags and dragged them into the bedroom. In front of the dresser, I cleared off all her stuff and sent everything crashing into the same trash bag.

"Wanna play me? Oh, I'ma show you just how I do it," I snapped as bottles and tubes crashed and cracked in the bag. But I didn't care. I wanted her and everything that might remind me of her gone. Everyone had warned me against Paisley, saying she would hurt me. But I didn't listen. Now I was paying with my heart.

When I finished filling the fourth trash bag, I stood back and took a visual inventory of the closet and the bedroom. I had to admit, it looked empty without her stuff, but I was confident life would go on once she was gone.

One at a time, I pulled the bags to the top of the stairs and tied them the best I could. When I was confident they were secure, I shoved them down the stairs.

Paisley jumped up and ran to the stairs at the sound of bottles cracking.

"What are you doing?"

"I want you and your stuff out of here. This ain't no place for trash!" That said, I shoved the third bag down the stairs.

"Are you crazy? Are those my things I hear breaking up in those bags?"

"Probably." I pushed the last bag down and stood there, daring her to say something else about it.

"You can't be serious. I made a mistake. I should've called. But nothing happened. Why are you doing this?"

I cocked my head to one side and tried to give her time to answer that herself.

"Go back to wherever the hell you've been for the past three days. I don't want your ass anymore."

"What are you saying? How could you be so cold, so callous," she shrieked, "without even hearing me out?"

I was about to turn and walk away when I thought about her question.

"You ain't seen nothin' yet. I suggest you take your trash and get out of my sight before things really get ugly around here."

In a stance of defiance, she threw her hands to her hips and asked, "So where am I supposed to go?"

"Go back to that nigga. I don't care where you go, to tell the truth. All I know is when I come out of my room, I want you gone! Hell. Go to Trina's. Maybe y'all can go turn some tricks together."

I turned around and walked away before she could ask another question or make another statement. But I was sure images of her standing there with her tearstained face would haunt me long after she was gone.

18

Caleb

Ain't no sunshine when she's gone. I couldn't believe I couldn't get that stupid song out of my head. Hell, I couldn't figure out why these feelings were creeping up on me. What do I want with somebody who can't make up her mind between me and her ex? It had been two days since I'd put Paisley out and I still couldn't get her off my mind.

"Dang, boss. Somebody has done you real wrong. What happened? You found a roach in your salad at lunch or something?" Dedra asked with a smile etched across her face. I had walked past her desk heading back from lunch and just wanted to sulk in my office.

I watched her hips sway as she walked from the file cabinet back over to her desk and I tried to offer up a smile, but I'm sure it was weak.

"Nah, seriously," she said, sitting down behind her desk. "I'm just messing with you, but what's wrong? And don't even try and front by saying nothing. I've been working with you too long not to be able to tell when something is wrong. I'm not sure what, but something is written all over your face and it ain't pretty." She perched her elbows on top of her desk and held up her head. "So? Let's have it," she pressed.

I motioned toward my office with my head. "Give me five and we can talk." I continued on to my office.

"Five!" she yelled as I closed my door. I needed to pull myself together, and I needed to do it quickly. Paisley was getting to me in the worst way possible.

Looking around the office, I couldn't avoid seeing pictures of the two of us. Those were happier times, of course, but now they stood as staunch reminders of what could've been.

Our time together might have been short, but I really had seen a future with Paisley. Okay, now I'm starting to sound like some weak little punk. I was glad when Dedra walked into my office.

She plopped herself onto the sofa and patted the spot next to her.

"Come talk to Mama," she joked.

I smiled and shook my head.

"Dang, it's about time. I was starting to worry for real. A smile means there is still some hope left." She patted the seat again. "Seriously now, come over here. Carla is covering the phones, so we got as much time as you need."

I pulled myself over to where she sat and eased my body onto the sofa. It was as if I was relieving myself of a massive load. Dedra reached over and tried to rub my shoulders, but my position wouldn't allow it.

"Here, turn around so I can help you relieve some of this stress." She firmly squeezed my shoulders. "Dang, it's all hard up there. What's really going on, Caleb? Before you start, here, turn around." She adjusted herself onto the arm of the sofa and pulled me back between her legs.

"Don't worry. I locked your door," she said when she noticed me eyeing it.

I relaxed. Dedra was always taking care of everything. I rested both arms on her thighs. That's when I caught sight of her ring finger. I took her hand.

"Wh-what's that?"

She quickly pulled her hand away. "What does it look like?"

I turned around and looked at her. "It looks like an engagement ring."

"Then I guess that's what it would be," she said as she tried to turn me back around.

"So old Marcus finally popped the question," I said, referring to her boyfriend of a year and a half.

"Yep."

"Dang, don't sound so excited. I thought you were breaking up with him anyway."

"We worked it out. Now turn around."

I could tell she didn't want to talk about it. Dedra always had been secretive about her private life. In all her time with me, I'd seen only one man she'd ever dated, and that was Marcus, with his nerdy behind.

"Unbutton your shirt," Dedra ordered.

"I like a woman who takes control," I joked.

"Be quiet, and unbutton your shirt," she responded.

I rested both arms on her thighs and closed my eyes. "I know you ain't trying to take advantage of a brotha while he's down, are you?"

"Boy, if you don't lean back here and unbutton that shirt . . ." She playfully popped me upside the head. I reluctantly did as I was told.

About twenty minutes into the massage and therapy session, I had nearly finished my story about Paisley and how she spent the weekend with some other man. I know I probably shouldn't have been as relaxed with Dedra since she was my secretary, but she was more than that, she was a friend. And even though we were so close, she knew how and when to keep it professional.

"Why didn't you let her explain?"

"There was nothing to explain."

"Maybe she didn't have sex with him."

"And maybe I got the winning lotto numbers. She slept with him. And even if she didn't, she spent the weekend with another man while I was sitting at home, worried sick. It's bad enough she didn't want to sign the prenup, but then she gon' try and play me with another man."

"You know, you and this professional mentality," Dedra mumbled.

"What is that supposed to mean?" I turned my head to the side so she could work out the knot in my shoulder.

"It means Paisley and every other woman you're with ain't some big deal you negotiated. As an investment banker you're always trying to control something, looking at the long term, investing into her, hoping your investment will pay off. Instead of just loving her and taking the relationship for what it's worth, you gotta come with stipulations, addenda to a contract of love."

I chuckled. "Okay, Dedra, that's a bit much. The bottom line is Paisley did me wrong."

"Maybe. Maybe not." Dedra's hands felt good against my skin. "But can I ask you a question?"

"Shoot."

"If you are so convinced that she did you wrong, even though you wouldn't listen to her explanation, why are you walking around here acting like you lost the very best thing to ever happen to you?"

I had to think about that one for a minute. When I was sitting up in the dark, waiting for Paisley like a madman, I was so angry I just wanted to squeeze the life out of her. Then, by the time she snuck into the house and I could see the distress across her face, it made me even more disgusted with the way she was trying to play me. I was torn, because I wanted to take her into my arms and fix her troubles, but the other part of me was, like, what kind of fool would I be to let her walk all over me?

Shoving her things into those trash bags made me feel somewhat vindicated, because it was as if I was in control. But the second I heard the front door close, I knew it was for the last time. Then I saw the key sitting on the coffee table, and I've had this sinking feeling in the pit of my stomach ever since and it hasn't gone away.

"You're not going to answer the question?" Dedra's voice brought me back to the conversation.

"I guess it's because I just knew that she may be the one."

Silence fell over us. I debated against letting Dedra see me act all heartbroken, but it's funny, Dedra was the only person on this earth I felt I could just be myself with.

"I mean, Paisley was the one, Dedra."

She stopped massaging my neck. "Caleb, how many times have you said that? Every girl you date is *the one.* You want this perfect woman to give you unconditional love, yet you continue to put conditions on love."

Dedra paused and blew a frustrated breath.

I turned to face her. "Man, you're getting a little worked up."

She sighed. "Caleb, it's because I keep watching you do the same thing, make the same mistakes, over and over. It's like you're not learning from any of your past mistakes. You're not growing in your relationships and the way you approach them." She shook her head, then turned my body back around.

"Just forget it. If you still love Paisley, why are you suffering? Why not go and get her back? It makes no sense. You said yourself she didn't want to leave, so go and work things out." It sounded like she didn't really mean that, but I chalked it up to my imagination. Her words were really hitting home. If I keep getting the same results in all of my relationships, maybe it's me who's doing something wrong.

"You make getting back with Paisley sound so simple."

Dedra took a deep breath as she gently pushed me up and stood. "It is, if you think about it. I don't know what Paisley was doing when she was away from you, but the bottom line is, she came back home."

I jumped up. "So now I'm just supposed to be some kind of punk and let her walk all over me, right? I may love her, but I ain't gonna be nobody's fool. It's just that simple. I don't care how fine she is, how perfect we'd be together, my woman is gonna respect me and our relationship or she needs to move on to the next man, and I mean that." I know I was sounding a little forceful, but I had so many mixed emotions running through me, I didn't know what to think.

"Whoa!" Dedra held her hands up. "I didn't mean to set you off. I'm not trying to make you any more upset than you already are. All I'm saying is, I don't want to see you moping around here if there's something you can do to fix things."

I sighed, my bravado fading. "Dedra, I thought we understood each other. What about the fact that she made a complete fool of me? Don't you understand? She treated me like crap, made a straight fool out of me, and you expect me to take her back?" I huffed.

Dedra looked up at me with sad puppy eyes. "We're all somebody's fool at some point in our lives," she mumbled.

Before I could ponder that, my desk phone buzzed. Both of us looked at it, then I jumped up and answered the intercom.

"Caleb here," I said.

"Caleb, it's Cook. We've got major problems with the Stackhouse account." I groaned. I had worried that we might have some issues with that account since I was supposed to meet with Mr. Stackhouse the day I put Paisley out. I'd gotten so caught up in the drama with Paisley that I'd completely forgotten about the meeting. Mr. Stackhouse had not been happy that I missed the meeting and he was even more upset because he said the documents I'd sent him looked sloppy.

"Oh?" I looked at Dedra, wondering if she knew whether Mr. Cook was aware that I had missed the meeting. She shrugged her shoulders.

"Yeah, Smith is calling for your ass on a platter, and I have to be honest. After reviewing these documents, I'm gonna need a whole lot of reasons from you about why I shouldn't agree. Then on top of that, Jerroll Hunt signed with another firm today. I thought you had that in the bag."

My head suddenly felt light, and my throat went dry. The other partner, Mr. Smith, was a no-nonsense businessman.

"Did you or did you not sign that deal?" Cook demanded.

"Well, I, um . . . well, when I left, he assured me he would sign the papers."

"You mean you didn't personally have him sign them?" Mr. Cook's voice bellowed through the phone.

"Well, I, ah—"

"I need to see you in my office *right now!*" He slammed down the phone.

I silently cursed as I scrambled to button my shirt. Now Paisley wasn't only messing with my mind, she was messing with my job. And that simply couldn't happen.

Dedra could tell by the frazzled look on my face that I was in major trouble.

"Is there anything I can do?" she asked.

"Naw, I got it." I scrambled toward my boss's office, praying I could straighten all of this out before it was too late.

19

Paisley

When I stepped out of my car and looked down the street, I was amazed by how much things had remained the same over the years. There were still no sidewalks, people's yards were still crowded with trash or empty beer bottles and cans, and the grass was dried out and dead. Gone were the neatly manicured lawns and sprawling, single-family homes made of brick and fancy designs.

I looked at my mother's old wooden house sitting on bricks and got this sinking feeling all over again.

Before I could cross the street, two kids riding the same bike nearly ran right into me.

"Watch it, lady," one screamed while balancing the other on the handlebars. I didn't even bother responding.

Since I couldn't park in my mother's little piece of a yard because it was littered with broken-down cars and other vehicles, I had to park in front of another yard and hope for the best. Walking up to the rickety little fence, I noticed the three overflowing trash cans that looked like they'd been sitting out longer than the city of Houston should permit.

"Is that you, Paisley?"

I looked over at the side of the other house and noticed Miss Betty. She was hunched over, sitting on a milk crate that had been pulled up to an old card table.

"Yes, Miss Betty, it's me. How are you?"

She sighed, and I rolled my eyes. "Well, baby, my arthritis is acting up. My Medicaid done stopped doing what it was 'posed to do, so I can't pay for my meds, and I can't keep my things nailed down good enough to stop Eugene from selling off my stuff."

She was referring to her grown son, who had been on drugs for years and was in and out of jail and living with her in between his stints of freedom.

"Oh, well, I'm sorry to hear all of that." I pulled on the fence that looked as if it were held together with large rubber bands.

"Yeah, chile, I can't wait for Eugene to see you. I used to tell that boy you were goin' places. Now look atcha, driving a nice, fine car, wearing all those fancy clothes. You done did good for yourself. I can see that from here, and you know my damn cataracts just messing up my eyes."

"Cataracts?" I don't even know why I asked.

"Oh yes, baby. Doctor said he may need to take the right one." She leaned back, using an old newspaper to fan herself. "Oooh, wee, chile, sure is hot out here!"

"Okay, well, Miss Betty, I need to get on inside, but I'll be seeing you around."

"How long you staying, baby? I mean, you got all them bags," she said.

"Oh, this stuff?" I smiled and looked down as if just realizing the load I was packing. "I'm bringing some things for Mama," I lied. I had stayed at Trina's for the past two nights, but she was having her place remodeled and had moved in with her beau of the moment for the next four weeks. I didn't have any place to go but here.

"Umph, well, I can't wait for Eugene to see you. I suspect he'll be here directly," she said.

"Okay, well, tell him hello for me." I smiled and quickly stepped into the yard and up the little wooden step. I had to move carefully to avoid having my heel sink into one of the many rotten holes.

The minute I stepped into the small, dark house, I could feel my skin begin to crawl. The air was hot and muggy despite the window unit, which was blowing air with great force.

"Ma!" I cried.

I could hear something frying in the kitchen. The smoke didn't do much to help with the already musty smell that permeated the small room.

My mother stuck her head out from behind the wall that separated the small kitchen from the living room.

"Paisley, baby, that you? What you doin' 'round these parts?" She came out and rubbed her hands on her apron as she started waving the smoke away. "Sorry 'bout all this doggone smoke. I swear, sometimes I just don't know," she hissed, still fanning the air.

"Now come on in here in the light. Let me get a good look at you," she said, walking over to hug me.

"Ma, I'd rather not. I don't want to get that smoke all in my hair and clothes." I held my mother tightly, missing her and feeling bad for not being able to help her live in a better environment.

When we pulled away, I marveled at the old pictures of me hanging on the walls. It was like a hall of fame dedicated to different phases of my life. Two small, plastic-covered sofas were spaced evenly on opposite sides of the room, and one of those old-fashioned floor-model TVs served as a stand for a smaller, more modern TV. It was on, but the volume was turned down. When Mama went back into the kitchen, I knew exactly what I had to do. I had to do better, not just for me, but for her.

I picked up the phone and dialed Caleb's office. When he answered, my mind went blank.

"Hello?"

I wanted to speak, but I couldn't bring myself to say the words.

"Hello?"

"Caleb, baby?"

He didn't respond.

"I'm sorry, and I want to come home. I wanna come back to you, baby. I miss you, and I'm so sorry. Can't we try to work this out?"

My heart sank when there was still silence on the other end of the line.

"Look," he finally said, "I'm having a rough day at work. I can't deal with you."

"Wait," I said before he hung up. "Can I please come over? Just to talk. Then I'll leave you alone forever." I had no intention of leaving him alone. Being back here in my mother's house, with smoke filling my nose, reminded me that I *couldn't* leave him alone. I had to do whatever it took for Caleb to take me back.

He hesitated. "Whatever, Paisley."

I wanted to turn a backflip. "What time will you be home?"

He paused again. "I'll be there by seven." He slammed the phone down before I could say another word. I smiled as I grabbed my bags, took them to my car, then went back inside to spend a few minutes with my mother.

20

Caleb

I could tell from the look on Paisley's face she was happy to be back. Truth be told, so was I. We had sex before we said a word. It was absolutely phenomenal. But now that we were sitting in my bed, Paisley had tears in her eyes.

I didn't know what to say, but I knew we couldn't pretend that nothing happened. "Where were you?"

"I was in Jamaica with Bobby."

She could've knocked me over right there. I mean, I knew it, but to hear her say it was heartbreaking.

"I couldn't talk because he was always around."

I looked at her as if she had lost her mind. Any hope I had of us working this out was quickly waning.

"I—I had never been to Jamaica. Had always dreamed about it but never could afford to go. Me and Bobby came up on some money one time when we were together and bought a time-share, and it was about to expire. I just wanted the experience and I didn't want to lose my thousand dollars."

Now I knew she was crazy. I got up from the bed and began

pacing the floor. "Tell me you went for closure. Tell me you went to make sure you were over him. Don't say you went for a thousand dollars. I'd have given you a thousand dollars."

"It wasn't just about the money." She wept. "You're right about the closure thing. I had to make sure I didn't have any lingering feelings. I mean, we're talking about marriage. I just needed to know."

I wanted to tell her to get out, right then and there. Instead, I said, "So do you know?"

She stood up. "Without a shadow of a doubt. Caleb, I only want to marry one time. And every part of me is telling me you're the man for me, but this prenup thing is messing with me. It's obvious you don't trust me and so that has me wondering can we really make it if there's no trust. So all that stuff is racing through my mind and Bobby comes along and, I don't know, I guess I couldn't go forward until that part of my life was completely closed."

I glared at her. "Did you sleep with him?"

"No. I swear. I didn't let him touch me."

"Y'all sleep in the same bed?"

"No, I made him get double beds."

I didn't know what to believe. "He didn't try anything?"

"He tried, but I said no. And besides, I was on my cycle."

This shit was making absolutely no sense to me. "I can't deal with this, Paisley."

"Just give me another chance."

I spun on her. "For what? So you can do this again?"

She looked at me with tear-filled eyes. "Just let me hold you."

"What do you think holding me is gon' do?"

Her arms wrapped around me like a soft octopus, walking me back to the bed. I wanted to curse her out, but I let her hands roam all over my body instead.

She lowered me onto my bed, gently planting kisses all over me. "Caleb, I love you. Only you. I know that now more than ever." She kissed me like she was trying to erase everything in my mind. She was doing a damn good job.

I guess that's why they say make-up sex is the best sex. That was the best fifty-seven minutes of my life.

When all was said and done, I realized I would forgive her. I really believed her when she said she didn't sleep with him. Maybe I was the crazy one, but I guess I wanted to believe her. So forgive her, yes. But I'd never forget. I just told myself I wouldn't bring that shit up again. Only I had no idea how hard that was going to be.

21

Caleb

It was like she never left. Paisley and I had drifted right back into our groove. I tried to stay mad at her, but she made it so hard.

I was standing in the kitchen, buck naked, looking through the refrigerator for something to drink. As I grabbed a glass of water, my phone rang.

After a quick sip, I answered it when I saw Todd's number.

"What's up?"

"You, man. You by yourself?"

"Yeah, Paisley's in the room, knocked out. You know a brotha be wearing them out." I laughed, surprised at how good I was feeling.

"Whatever. As your best friend, I felt it was my duty to call you before she whipped it on you and you lost all common sense."

"What you gotta warn me about?"

"Don't get caught up, man."

"What is that supposed to mean?" My laughter died down.

"It means just 'cause y'all got back together and she sexing you up and shit, don't let her sucker you into forgetting about that prenup."

The prenup. That damn piece of paper was becoming the bane of my existence.

"Man, I haven't forgotten about the prenup."

"Okay, I'm just checking," Todd said.

"Well, you ain't gotta worry."

"A'ight, man. Peace."

I hung up the phone and almost dropped my water at the sight of Paisley standing in the living room, her sheer robe hanging open, exposing her perfectly sculpted body. I was just about to try to explain my conversation, but the way she smiled and slithered toward me, she must not have heard it.

"Ummmm, baby, we need to break up more often." She ran her fingers over my chest, across my nipples, and down my rock-hard stomach. "I want to feel you inside me again."

I leaned in and kissed her. Maybe she did hear and this was her way of trying to keep me offtrack. I wasn't about to let that happen. "As much as I would love to take you right here on the kitchen counter, we need to get a few things straight."

She took a step back, the smile leaving her face.

I took her hand and led her into the living room. She looked bewildered as I sat her down on the sofa. "Babe, I'm glad we agreed to work this out. But nothing's changed."

"What is that supposed to mean?"

"It means what it means."

"Caleb, just say what you are trying to say."

I could tell she was getting an attitude, so I had to tread lightly. "I still want to marry you."

"But . . . ?"

"But I still need a prenup."

"Oh, here we go with this bullshit." She huffed and rolled her eyes.

"It's not bullshit to me, Paisley. I don't understand what the big deal is. If you're not after me for my money, why won't you sign it?"

"Because a prenup is basically a way of saying, 'I know this relationship isn't gonna work and sign this for when it doesn't.' I mean, this is stupid. We haven't even set a date yet, and you talking to me about a damn prenup."

"We haven't set a date because I don't have a prenup." I let out a frustrated sigh. "You know what? I don't want to have this argument again. No prenup, no wedding. That's the bottom line."

"Just like that, huh, Caleb? Fuck discussing anything."

I stood up. "I'm not doing this with you, Paisley. I'm ready to give you the world. But if you can't do this, maybe we need to rethink this altogether." I stared at her. She had tears in her eyes. For once, I wasn't moved. I was serious about this. "I'm going back to bed."

I left her in the middle of the living room, fighting back tears.

22

Paisley

"That fool did *what?*"

I should've known Trina was going to hit the roof. I contemplated not telling her at all, but I needed to vent so bad that I left Caleb's and headed straight over to her boyfriend's place, where she was staying. "He gave me an ultimatum."

"You oughta ulti his matum. Tell that nigga to be gone." Trina handed me the phone. "Here."

"Girl, I'm not fixin' to call Caleb."

"Well, call Bobby."

"Bobby? For what?"

"Tell him you're suddenly single." She flung the phone down when I didn't take it. "Please, Bobby got more money than Caleb anyway. I don't know why you're even fooling with him. I can't stand arrogant, six-figga niggas, think they can treat people any ol' way. You need to show him you are a woman with options."

That said, Trina plopped down on the sofa. You'd have thought she was the one being forced to sign a prenup.

"Maybe I should just sign it," I woefully remarked.

"Maybe you should stop smoking that crack that is obviously destroying your brain cells," she snapped.

"Trina, I love Caleb, I really do. Yes, his money piqued my interest, but I really love him and I want to spend the rest of my life with him. The money doesn't matter . . . I think."

"Screw that Oprah bullshit. You know what a life of poverty is like. Hell, we both know. It ain't pretty. Neither of us is trying to go back to that. There is nothing wrong with wanting something better."

"I know." I nodded. "The fact that I love Caleb proves I can love a rich man just like I can a broke one."

"Hell, yeah. Who wants a broke man anyway?" Trina shook her head. "I mean, you are a good woman. You deserve the finer things in life. And you deserve a man who is willing to give that to you."

"But seriously, why am I entitled to his money?"

Trina let out an exasperated sigh. "Because when you marry him, that means you will have to give COD."

"What's that?"

"Coochie on demand. Not to mention, he's going to want you to clean, cook, be the perfect little trophy wife. Let's not even get started on the kids. Your dreams and aspirations will have to take a backseat to him. That shit costs, Paisley. And you sign that prenup, do all that, then look up ten, twenty years from now after your titties start sagging, your hips fill out, and Caleb wants to move on to the next pretty young thang. Where will that leave you? With what he feels like giving you. I don't think so."

I hadn't thought about that.

"Do you want to end up like Lydia Collings?"

"Who's that?"

"That lady who lives next door to your mom. You know, the

one who had to move in that shack after her doctor husband left her. Remember, she signed a prenup. And she's still fighting to get five dollars. Her husband was mad because she wouldn't take his funky twenty-thousand-dollar settlement. Now he won't give her anything. Do you want to be like that? Do you want to have to move back to Fifth Ward when Caleb gets tired of you?"

I was speechless. I had forgotten all about Lydia. She moved back when I was in high school. That was the first time I'd ever heard of a prenup. Her husband got custody of their son, and she was left with nothing. She was the most miserable person I ever met, and she even had to go on welfare just to make ends meet. Oh hell no, that would never be me.

"Paisley, I'm just saying, you need to convince Caleb that a prenup is *not* the answer. And if he remains adamant, screw him. Move on."

I weighed everything Trina was saying and another thought popped up in my mind—one I'd been pushing to the back of my mind for years.

"Trina, there's something else." I hesitated, ignoring the look of exasperation on Trina's face. "You remember that little situation with Reginald, my ex?"

"What situation?"

"The photos?"

A wide smile crossed her face. "Oh dang. I forgot about those."

"That's nothing to smile about." I ran my fingers through my hair. What was I thinking? I was giving Caleb a hard time and I had issues of my own.

Trina waved me off. "Please, that ain't nothing to be worried about. Worry about that prenup."

"But what if he finds out?" Caleb was definitely on the fast track, with us, with work. I would hate for those stupid pictures to resurface and ruin everything.

"He won't,' Trina said matter-of-factly. "Didn't you tell me Reginald got married?"

I nodded.

"Well, then. Trust he ain't trying to let those photos come out. Besides, what Caleb doesn't know won't hurt him."

I sighed heavily. As much as I loved Trina, maybe I shouldn't be listening to her. I had so much swirling in my mind. This prenup. How furious Caleb would be if he knew my secrets. He would definitely use that to bolster his argument about the prenup. That's if he could even forgive me at all.

"Listen," Trina said, turning serious. "It's been how many years since you took those pictures?"

"A few years," I said softly.

"And they haven't come up yet. So quit trippin'. You have the upper hand in this relationship and you need to keep it that way."

I sighed. Maybe Trina was right, at least about the not worrying part. It had been a while and I hadn't so much as heard from Reginald. I took a deep breath and pushed thoughts of the photos to the back of my mind. I needed to be focused on the prenup. I really and truly didn't want Caleb just for his money, but I wasn't a fool either. Nope, we'd just have to figure out something because I was determined to get my man, and I was going to get him without a prenup.

23

Caleb

"Uggggh!" I slammed the phone down and buried my face in the palm of my hands. I just needed to forget all about the Stackhouse account. It was what it was, that was all there was to it. Mr. Stackhouse was still pissed with a capital *P*, and there wasn't anything I could do about it. I'd just spent the past hour trying to convince him not to pull his account, and it wasn't looking good. After Jerroll signed with another firm, I didn't need to lose this account as well.

I pressed the button to bring my computer to life. I just needed to escape. I'd been sitting here sulking over the mess of that account and trying to go over in my mind how to deal with Paisley.

First, I checked my e-mail to make sure I wasn't ignoring anything urgent on the work front. When there was nothing new there, I went to the search engine Google. I was going to do a search of couples who had either benefited or suffered from prenups.

I was just about to type in "prenup" when something made me pause. "Hmmm, I wonder. . . ." I looked toward the door just to make sure no one would pop in on me goofing off, then I typed in Paisley's name and watched as the little hourglass turned over, indicating the search was under way. I didn't know why I hadn't thought to do this before. Todd was always talking about checking people out on the Internet. I frowned when Paisley's name popped up on the screen. It was spelled two different ways.

I clicked on one and waited again.

"What the—" I could hardly believe my eyes. Plastered across my screen were several pictures of Paisley! And they weren't the kind of pictures you shared with your friends. One had her hanging on a pole from behind with nothing on but a string and the pole, of course separating her cheeks.

"Oh hell, naw!" I uttered as I clicked on another thumbnail.

This one had her spread out like an eagle on a rug with whipped cream strategically covering both breasts and her crotch. The smile on her face was hard to ignore.

"Add Paisley to your party and she's sure to spice things up" read the caption beneath the slew of explicit pictures of her.

I couldn't believe this! Of all the beautiful women in the city of Houston, I had to hook up with a former stripper. Ain't no tellin' how many other men had paid for this ass.

I buried my head in my hands again. "What else can happen here?"

I needed to straighten this mess out, so I immediately picked up the phone and called Paisley.

"Hi, baby," she said.

Part of me was relieved that she was no longer angry about the prenup issue, but then I quickly snapped back to the reason for my call. "Where are you?"

"Shopping. Why? You need something?" she asked sweetly.

"Yeah, meet me at the house in an hour!"

"Caleb? Is everything okay?"

I heard her, but I just hung up. I was pissed, but I wanted to give her a chance to explain, as if this could even be explained. I hit a button on the keyboard and watched as images of Paisley dissolved on the screen.

"If it ain't one damn thing, it's another." I got up, grabbed my briefcase, and stormed out of the office.

"Reach me on my cell. I'll be back in a few hours," I said grimly over my shoulder to Dedra as I rushed to the elevator.

I tried my best to calm myself before seeing Paisley's face, but when I pulled up and saw her car in the driveway, the googled images of her ass, her *bare* ass at that, flashed through my head. Shaking them off as best I could, I made my way to the door, took a deep breath, and then stepped inside.

"Baby, is that you?"

Soft music was playing, and I could hear the water running in the kitchen. I didn't even answer her.

When she stuck her head around the corner, her eyebrows shot up. "Are you okay?"

I looked at her and guessed that my expression answered her question. She came into the living room and attempted to hug me. In disgust, I pulled her arms from my neck and walked across the room.

"Caleb, I don't know what's bothering you, but we can't fix it if we don't at least try to communicate," she suggested.

"You wanna communicate?" I snickered. "Well, how about this. Tell me why I googled your ass, and your ass literally popped up on the screen. How about we communicate about *that,* Paisley?"

The color drained from her face, and she suddenly had to clear her throat.

"Oh, is that what this is all about?"

"Wrong answer, Paisley. I'm gonna need you to come stronger this time."

She shrugged. I could see embarrassment settle in her features. She was trying to act like it was no big deal, but I could tell she was rattled.

"You know I do modeling."

"Yeah! I thought, like, a Ford model, a runway model, hell, even a damn catalog model. Not a freakin' porn star!"

"I wasn't a porn star, Caleb." She sighed as she looked at me. "What do you want me to say?"

"How about, 'It wasn't me'? How about, 'Those were private pictures that fell into the wrong hands'? How about, 'I wasn't tryin' to sell my ass to the highest bidder'? How about something like that?" By then I was shaking. When I realized just how much, I tried to calm myself. I closed my eyes, waiting for her response.

"Okay, okay, Caleb. I can tell you anything you want to hear. You want me to say that wasn't me? It wasn't. You want me to say somebody did that to me? They did." She inched closer. I could smell her scent, and it pissed me off that I still wanted her.

"But none of that would be true. Look, baby, we've all done things we aren't proud of. There are things in my past I'm not proud of, but that's just what it is—it's my past, baby. That's *not* the woman who's standing before you today. That's *not* the woman who wants to spend the rest of her life with you."

I opened my eyes and looked at her. "Why, Paisley?"

"Because I had to eat. Because I was broke. Because I needed to survive. I had to take care of myself and my mother, that's why, Caleb. Am I proud of the things I've had to do to survive?" She shook her head. "No, I'm not, but I would've thought you, of all people, would understand that the things we did in the past shouldn't determine or dictate who we are today."

"So you used to take your clothes off for money?" I swallowed hard, still not wanting to believe what my eyes had seen or what my ears were hearing.

She slowly nodded her head. "Yes, Caleb, I used to be a stripper. But I only did private parties. I had an upscale clientele, and it was all about the money. I never cared about any of those men and women."

My eyes widened. "Men *and* women?"

"Here." She kissed me. "I'm tired of talking," she said, biting my lip softly.

Despite my anger, something stirred. I couldn't fight it. She took me into her arms and gently stroked my head, shoulders, and back.

The taste of her lips was so enticing. I quickly felt my nature rising. It was like she was sucking the rage and anger right out of my body as she held my tongue between her lips and caressed it with her own.

"Paisley, this isn't always the answer!" I said in between breaths as she tore at my clothes. She ignored my protests and within seconds stood in front of me in all her glory, her beautiful body begging me for satisfaction.

"I love you, Caleb. I don't want to remember my past. Only my future." She turned and sashayed over to the coffee table.

Shoving the stuff off, she straddled it, inched her legs up, and laid on her back. "Are you gonna just stand there and watch?"

I was so hard, I thought I was about to explode. Why did my body keep betraying my mind? I walked over, got on my knees, and entered her with such force, her eyes bucked. She wrapped her legs around me and pulled me in deeper.

"Go deeper, baby. It's all yours, I promise!" she cried.

I plunged into her again, trying desperately to forget that, once more, she was using sex to try to solve our problems—problems that I felt were far from over.

24

Paisley

I laughed as I watched the cowboy on our forty-two-inch flat screen yell, "There's gold in them there hills."

That's how I felt. I was packing pure, fourteen-karat gold. And I'd just used it all on Caleb. I made him forget all about the stripping, and it was just a matter of time before he forgot about the prenup as well. Trina was so right. There was power in the poontang.

Despite the fact that I'd convinced Caleb to let the issue drop, I still felt bad.

Caleb had just left to go work out. I was walking around the house in my robe as I filled the Jacuzzi tub with steaming hot water, made my way into the kitchen, and then poured myself a glass of wine.

I savored the liquid as it slid down my throat. I couldn't believe I had been so stupid as to pose for those pictures. But when you're young and dumb, you do things without thinking, especially when you are as broke as I was. I just hoped Caleb believed me. I really did love him, and I wanted desperately for our relationship to work. Hell, I *needed* it to work. I had only stripped for about two months, trying to make ends meet. I had never intended to do that in the first place, but Reginald, the guy I was dating at the time, convinced me it was an easy way to make some quick cash.

I got out because even though I worked with upscale clients, I couldn't take some man pawing all over me for a few dollars. That picture Caleb saw was for a calendar one of my clients had done. I knew the pictures were out there but I had no idea they were posted on the Internet.

My ringing cell phone interrupted my thoughts. I groaned when I saw Bobby's number and debated about not answering it, but I knew he would just keep calling.

"Yes?" I said, snapping it open.

"What are you wearing?"

I looked nervously around, like he was spying on me or something. "What do you want, Bobby?"

"You."

"Bobby, I told you, I'm with Caleb now."

"Yeah, your mouth told me that. But your body, whenever it's near me, it tells me something else."

I shifted uncomfortably, wondering why in the hell this man still had any kind of effect on me. "Bobby, I don't care what you think my body is saying to you. I'm telling you, I love my man and there's nothing you can say or do to change that."

"Nothing?"

"Nothing."

"Go open your front door."

"My front door? I don't live in my old place anymore."

"I know where you live. In Caleb's itty-bitty condo. Remember, that's where I picked you up for our trip to Jamaica. Now, open the front door."

He definitely had my interest piqued. "Bobby, I don't have time to play games with you."

"Just open the door, Paisley."

I did what he said and looked down to find a small gold box with a red ribbon around it.

"Do you have the door open?"

"Yes." I leaned down to pick up the box, pushing my shoulder up to hold the phone while I tried to open the box. After pulling the ribbon off, I quickly removed the top. "What is this?"

"What does it look like?"

I could tell he was enjoying this.

"It looks like a key."

"Then it's a key. Now, walk downstairs."

"Bobby, I have bathwater running, and I'm about to get in the tub."

"This will only take a minute. Don't you want to know what the key is to?"

I sighed as I set the box down, slipped my tank top back over my head, ran and cut the water off, then headed downstairs. "What am I looking for, Bobby?"

"What's in the fire zone?"

I looked around. "I don't see anything . . . but a silver Bentley."

"I wonder if that key fits it."

I almost dropped the phone. "Oh, my God!" I said as I positioned the phone back to my ear and raced over to the car. As soon as I put the key near the door, the car automatically unlocked.

"Bobby, what is this?" I excitedly asked as I climbed in the car.

"It's my car."

"Why do you have your car parked outside my place?"

"Caleb's place," he corrected me. "And my car is now your car. It's my way of saying congratulations on your engagement, and I'm sorry for all the drama I put you through when we were together."

I ran my hand along the soft leather seats. "Bobby, what are you talking about?"

"I bought the car when I got my first major client. And I've upgraded now, thanks to yet another client signing a very lucrative endorsement deal. So I decided, instead of just letting the Bentley sit in my garage, I wanted to give it to someone who deserved it."

I couldn't say anything. Bobby always did have a good heart. He just never had the money to go along with it.

"I know I cheated on you, Paisley. But I was dumb and caught up. That's the biggest mistake I ever made and I wanted to give you this gift to say I'm sorry, I love you, and please accept this for all that you did for me when we were together."

"Bobby . . ."

"Ssssh . . . don't say anything, baby. Just take the gift. Turn on the CD player and let that Heather Headley CD play, particularly 'In My Mind.' I know you say another man has your heart, but you will always have mine. You will always belong to me, even if it's only in my mind. I couldn't give you much of anything except heartache when we were together. Take this car as a way of me making that up to you. I will always love you, Paisley."

Before I could respond, Bobby hung up the phone. I sat in the car, totally stunned. Tears were filling my eyes. Never in a million years did I dream I could have something like this.

I was still sitting there, running my hands over the steering wheel, when I heard Caleb's voice. "Paisley?"

I jumped and pushed the CD player off. "Hey, Caleb."

He scanned the car. "What is this?"

I turned off the engine, eased out, and slowly shut the door.

"Did you hear me, Paisley? Whose Bentley is this?" he asked when I didn't respond.

"It's—it's—ummm, mine."

Caleb shifted his gym bag on his shoulder. "Come again?"

I lowered my gaze. "It's mine. I mean, it's an engagement gift."

He raised his eyebrows. "You wanna tell me who the hell would give you a Bentley and why?"

All of my joy at receiving the car was slowly fading. "It's a gift from Bobby," I said softly. I had briefly contemplated lying but was trying to do things right with Caleb, and that meant no more lies.

Caleb looked like he was trying to contain his anger. "I hope you told Bobby what he can do with his Bentley."

It was my turn to look at Caleb as if he were crazy. "Give it back?"

"I didn't stutter."

Caleb turned and stormed toward the condo. I pushed the lock button on the car and quickly followed.

"Caleb, can we talk about this?"

"Hell, naw. Ain't nothing to talk about." He pushed his way into the house.

"It's not like he out-and-out bought it. He got a new car and gave me his old one."

"Paisley, come on. Ain't nothing old about this car."

"Caleb, it's not that big of a deal. It's just an engagement gift." I knew I was grasping at straws. It sounded crazy even to me. But this was a dream car, even if it was used.

"An engagement gift is for the both of us. I doubt very seriously this Bentley is intended for me." Caleb threw his bag down and turned to me. "And what the hell are you giving him in exchange for that car?"

"I'm not giving him anything," I protested.

"Unh-unh. A man doesn't give you a hundred-thousand-dollar car without expecting something in return. Were you planning to sleep with him?"

"Caleb, you're being ridiculous. Of course not."

"I don't know. You sitting here all giddy and shit. Like the BMW 550 I bought ain't good enough."

"Is that what this is about—car envy?" I smirked. Then I flinched because Caleb actually looked like he wanted to hit me.

He inhaled deeply. "You know what? Bottom line, any woman of mine doesn't take a hundred-thousand-dollar car from another man. End of story." With that, he stormed into the bedroom before I could say another word.

I was still sitting in the living room sulking when he came stomping back. He had changed clothes.

"Where are you going?" I asked.

"Out." He grabbed his keys and stopped right before he reached the door. "You need to call your ex and tell him you're bringing the car back."

He didn't give me time to respond as he left, letting the door slam behind him. I took a deep breath myself as I flipped open my cell phone to tell Bobby I couldn't keep the car. But I hesitated, then closed the phone. I'd give the car back tomorrow. But first, I just had to take it for a spin. I was dying to show it to Trina.

After I changed and made it back outside, I eased into the car, thrilled about being behind the wheel of a luxurious ride like this, if only for one night.

25

Caleb

"Over here!" Damon stood and waved from his seat in the corner of the bar at Pappadeaux Seafood Kitchen. He and Todd were just about to accept another round when I walked up.

"Oh wait, my boy needs a drink too," he said to the waitress. "What you drinking, dawg?" Todd turned to me.

I shrugged. "Let me get a Crown and Coke," I replied, pulling up a chair and sitting down.

"Make that a double," Damon tossed in before she left.

I sighed.

"Damn, that bad, huh?" Todd said. "You sighing like you got the weight of the world on your back."

"Man, you don't even wanna know." I shook my head as if that could make my problems go away.

"C'mon, man, whassup? How'd it go down?"

I shot Damon a puzzled look after his question.

"Dawg, I had to tell him," Todd tried to defend himself as he shook his head. "I mean, your girl's ass is just hanging out there in cyberspace for anybody to see. Man, that's classic!" He and Damon exchanged dap.

"Both of y'all can kiss my ass."

They stopped laughing.

"Naw, dawg, seriously though, how did you handle that?" Todd said.

"I personally don't see a problem with it," Damon said, attempting to maintain a straight face. I looked at him, trying to determine if he was really serious.

"C'mon, Paisley's fine as hell. Got a banging body. Why not share that?" He shrugged. "That's all I'm saying."

"Well, obviously she felt the same way. But you know, it was all in the past. So I guess I gotta let it go." I took a sip of the drink that the waitress had just placed in front of me.

"Either that or let her go," Todd said, his eyebrow inching up. "Stop trying to be Captain Save a Ho."

"Man, you better watch that," I warned. "We worked it out, so just drop it, okay?"

"Yeah, Todd, drop it—like Paisley dropped her clothes," Damon said, fighting back a laugh.

"Oh, y'all got jokes." I downed the rest of my drink.

"Well, if you worked it out, why the long face?" Todd asked, finally seeing I wasn't in the mood to joke.

I eased back in the chair and shook my head. "Man, I don't know. I mean, I'm not sure what it is about Paisley, but it's still like there's something not quite right. I don't know what else to say about it."

I recognized the looks I was getting from both Damon and Todd and knew what they were thinking before either one managed to say a word.

"Maybe it's me," I offered up.

"Well, I'm glad you said it," Damon tossed in.

"Whatever, bruh," I countered.

"I'm just saying, you trying to make these women love you and you keep getting played. I mean, let's see, before Paisley, there was Asia and Kendra—"

"Asia didn't play me," I interrupted.

"Okay, one out of how many?" Damon continued. "Then there was Lattice, Vivian . . ." Damon acted like he was still thinking.

"Let's not forget Bambi," Todd helped remind us.

I couldn't help but smile at that one.

"But was Bambi fine or what?" I threw in.

Bambi was a beautiful aspiring actress who was always in character. Someone told her she looked like the actress Dorothy Dandridge, and she was hell-bent on living that lifestyle. My problem wasn't with that, but the fact that she couldn't separate fact from fiction and she had a voracious sexual appetite.

"Bambi?" Damon asked, looking like he was struggling to remember her.

"Yeah, you remember her. She'd act out every single thing, especially when she was telling a story. She'd act out each character, and of course let's not forget the way she constantly referred to herself in third person," Todd recalled.

I started laughing, because in order for us to have sex, Bambi would have to role-play. It was the only way she could get hers.

"See, that's what I'm talking about. Where do you find these women?" Damon said. "And that just proves my point. Stuff always happening to you. You got some of the best stories. I mean, that kind of stuff doesn't happen to average dudes like me."

"I don't know," I said, shrugging off his comments. But deep down, I really did wonder if they had a point. Could it be that *I* was the problem and not the women I seemed to attract? Maybe there was a reason I was even attracted to such women. Now they had me wondering.

I downed the rest of my second drink. This stuff was making my head hurt. Maybe it was me, I don't know. All I did know was I couldn't take too many more surprises from Paisley.

26

Paisley

"I am so trippin' off this car," Trina said as she walked around and closely inspected the Bentley. She had stopped by our condo to see the car since she wasn't home when I went by there last night. I was supposed to be taking the car back to Bobby when Caleb got off from work today.

"I mean, even though it's used and all, it's still tight," Trina continued. "But he know he coulda bought you a new car."

"Girl, I'm still trippin' that Bobby would just up and give me a car like this in the first place," I said. "He didn't have two nickels when we were together."

"Oh, trust me, I know that. Remember, I was the main one always asking why you was with that busta in the first place. You were always talkin' 'bout 'love conquers all,'" Trina said. "Screw that. Love can't conquer the lights getting cut off, you sittin' up in the dark talkin' 'bout 'I can't see you, but I love you.'"

I laughed. Trina never was happy about my relationship with Bobby. Growing up, Trina and I used to dream about our knights in shining armor who were going to come sweep us up out of the ghetto. We'd vowed that we would never live the poverty-stricken lives our mothers did. Our fathers had both abandoned us, and our mothers struggled like crazy. We'd made a pact that wouldn't be us. Trina always had been about the money. Me, I wanted the money too. But I wanted love with it as well.

"You were hanging on to Bobby's broke ass, and he cheated on you anyway," Trina continued. "If he'd been rich, at least you would've gotten something out of the deal," Trina said as she leaned in and looked at the interior of the car. "But I definitely have to give him his props now. This car ain't no joke."

Trina stood up, looked around the garage, then back at my ride. "I gotta give it to you; you just seem to luck up on the generous kind of brothas, girl." She walked into a nearby corner. "I've never seen a garage so clean. I mean, look at this. Caleb's got all kinds of organization going on around this camp. A person could actually live out here. You can tell he's got money, that's for sure," she determined with a nod of her head as she looked around.

"Oh yeah?" I said mindlessly as I sat in the driver's seat with the door open. We were listening to Mary J. Blige's new CD. "How can you tell someone has money just by inspecting the inside of his garage?"

"Okay, think about this." Trina turned. "He's got things organized in glass-enclosed cabinets, in the garage, girl. It's almost like he had this stuff made specifically for the garage. What poor person you know got the time or money to make sure his garage looks just as good as the inside of his house? Shoot, this even looks better than some people's houses ever will," she said, pulling open a drawer.

"You do have a point there. That's the thing about Caleb—he's very organized. I guess you could say he's meticulous, likes everything in its place."

"So tell me this," Trina said.

I looked over at her and stood, closing the car door with care.

"So how come he didn't care about you keeping the car Bobby bought for you?" she asked with her eyebrows scrunched together.

"Oh, trust me, he cares. I have to give it back."

"Give it back! Are you crazy?" Trina said.

"Caleb is my fiancé, and I have to respect that," I said unconvincingly.

"That's jacked up. And he's trying to see if you're worthy of his trust by signing a damn prenup? Give me a break. You got to trust that fool to part with this." She patted the hood.

"Trina, this is hard enough as it is. You're only making it harder," I replied. "I just need to be glad he doesn't know about all the other stuff Bobby bought. At least I can keep that."

Trina sucked her teeth. "Hmph. Better you than me, that's all I have to say, 'cause none of the stuff would be going back if it was me, especially this bad boy." She rubbed the car.

"That would be why you're single." Startled, we both jerked our heads up and looked at Caleb, who was standing in the doorway. I held my breath, wondering how much he'd heard.

Trina rolled her eyes. "Whatever, Caleb." She turned back to me. "On that note, I gotta go. 'Bye, Paisley."

Trina glared at Caleb one more time before walking out of the garage.

Caleb stood, staring at me. "So this isn't the only gift you got?"

I opened my mouth, but nothing would come out.

"You know what?" he said, holding up his hand. "Don't even bother with the lies. *All* of it goes back." He stormed past me and into the house.

"Caleb, you're being ridiculous."

I followed him inside. He stopped and spun around. "How would you like it if I was taking gifts from my ex? Would that bother you, Paisley?"

I saw that little vein popping again, which meant he was about to explode. Besides, he had a point. I'd be pissed if he was taking gifts from an ex-girlfriend.

"Fine, Caleb. I'll give everything back."

He looked at me sternly. "*Everything.*"

"Everything," I repeated.

I debated trying to reason with him some more but I could tell, no matter what, he wasn't hearing it. "Fine. I'll go box up the rest of the stuff."

"I'll be waiting right here, ready to go," he said through clenched teeth.

All the stuff Bobby had bought me in Jamaica—the earrings, the Gucci purse, the expensive perfume, I could deal with giving back all of that. But I couldn't believe I was giving back a Bentley. If this didn't prove I loved Caleb, nothing would.

27

Caleb

I could see her eyes peering at me in the rearview mirror, but I didn't care. When I said I wanted that fool to have all his stuff back, that's exactly what I meant. Paisley needs to know I mean business. Either she's gonna be with me or she's gonna be with him, and hanging on to his stuff is, in a sense, saying she wants to be with him.

I had started to calm down; that is, until we exited the freeway on Post Oak Boulevard. By then I was getting hotter by the minute the closer we got to Bobby's place because I was trying to figure out how the hell she even knew where he lived.

We pulled up in front of his building, and Paisley hesitated before climbing out of the car. When I walked up to her window, she hit a button to lower it.

"What now?" I asked.

She looked up at me and finally said, "I was just wondering if it's safe for us to park here." Her voice was laced with attitude.

I looked up at the sign above my head.

"It says loading and unloading only, but don't worry, we're

good. We won't be here long. We're just going to unload this box and give him back this car. C'mon!"

She rolled her eyes at me but still didn't move with the kind of urgency I wanted.

"Paisley, is there a problem?"

"Well, it's just that, I, um, I don't want the car to get towed," she answered.

I slammed my hand on the roof of the car, and she jumped. She was really trying me.

"Who cares if this car gets towed? Get his stuff and let's go! I'm tired of this crap, Paisley."

When I noticed her eyes pooling, I thought I was going to lose it. No, she wasn't about to sit here crying over a bunch of crap her ex bought for her. I shook my head.

"Okay, okay, I'm coming, I'm coming. It's just"—she sighed—"um, I need a moment, that's all," she murmured, her hands flapping as if she was trying to psych herself up to do the impossible. "I'm sorry. I know you're right. I need to give him back his stuff. I just, well, I just need a moment," she repeated.

I looked around, trying to calm myself. The doorman held the door open for someone and glanced our way. I wondered if he was about to call the police, thinking we were having a lover's quarrel or something. He nodded his head when we made eye contact.

"Cut the bullshit, Paisley. Grab this stuff and let's go," I demanded in the best no-nonsense tone I could muster.

"Okay." She sighed again. I could actually see her chest heaving up and down. "I'm ready," she announced. I moved back and pulled the door open for her.

She stepped out and placed her arms around my neck. With

our faces only inches apart, she gazed into my eyes and said, "I know this is the right thing to do. And I want you to know that this stuff means absolutely nothing to me if it puts any kind of doubt about us in your mind. You understand me?"

"That's exactly what it does," I assured her. She kissed my lips, seemingly relieved.

Once we separated, she looked at me and said, "Then let's go return his stuff so we can eliminate that doubt. I love you, Caleb, and that's why I'm with you."

With that, I squeezed her tightly and let go. Then I held the back door open as she pulled out the box that not only contained new stuff but some old stuff, obviously from their time together. Normally I would've done the gentlemanly thing and insisted on taking it up for her, but I couldn't. I just wanted all of that stuff out of my sight.

At the door, the doorman gave her a familiar look and nodded at me again.

"Good day, madam, sir," he said.

"We're here to see Mr. Trumane," Paisley said.

"Of course. He's expecting you," the doorman said, motioning for us to go over to the elevator. Once the doors closed, I turned to her.

"How is he expecting us?" I asked.

"I called and told him I was bringing the stuff back. Plus, I had to find out where he lived."

I didn't respond, instead just leaned back against the mirror in the elevator.

The elevator doors opened to plush carpet and wall-to-wall luxury. Even I had to admit the fool had some taste.

A massive bronze sculpture of a man loving a woman greeted us the moment we stepped into the marble foyer. Two steps down was the sunken living room, which was tastefully decorated with modern leather furniture. A massive projection-style flat screen hung from the ceiling and behind it was a floor-to-ceiling window with a brown tint.

"I'll be right down," I heard him say before I could see him. Paisley placed the box on a nearby table and came to stand next to me.

"Did you drop the car keys in there too?"

She dug into her purse.

"Oh yeah," she said, pulling them out. I rolled my eyes at her.

When I looked up, my nemesis was walking down a winding staircase that I hadn't noticed before.

"Paisley, you're looking as lovely as ever," he said, all but drooling over my woman.

"So you're the lucky man?" he continued, finally turning his gaze to me.

"Yeah, and we're here to bring your stuff back," I replied.

"Paisley, you understood that when I give, I give from the heart, right? All these gifts are simply because I was unable to do right by you for so long, because I was unable to give you the things a queen like yourself deserves," he said.

Paisley looked momentarily torn, but then quickly pulled herself together.

"No, I, um, I want you to have them back. I don't need them," she stammered.

"I don't understand," he offered softly, like I wasn't standing there. I couldn't take it anymore.

"Look, the bottom line is, I don't need you buying anything for *my* woman," I said.

"Come on, man, they're just material things. Paisley's worth all of this and then some."

"I know exactly what she's worth, and anything she needs or wants, I can buy for her. So you can keep this stuff, give it to charity, one of your other women, anything, but she's not keeping it, any of it," I snapped.

"Cool, whatever, man," he said nonchalantly.

Paisley looked sick, but I didn't care.

"Everything is over there in that box, along with some other things I've had for a while." She pointed at the box, her voice trembling as she spoke. "The keys are in there too."

"Okay, so that's it. Let's go," I said, taking Paisley by the arm. I hit the button I saw, hoping it was summoning the elevator. As the doors opened, the fool said, "Oh, by the way, how's the prenup situation working out for y'all? Now, Paisley, you know I would have never asked that sort of thing from you. It's a shame he doesn't give you that type of trust."

I couldn't move. I knew I couldn't have possibly heard what I thought I had just heard. I could feel my grip on Paisley's arm tightening, but I couldn't stop myself. Now her entire body shook. I all but shoved her into the waiting elevator and shot him a look of death as the doors closed on his smiling face.

"Please, say something," she mumbled as we climbed into my car.

I was far too angry for words. I couldn't believe she had been discussing our personal business with some other man, and not just another man but her ex, of all people. I didn't want to face it, but at that moment, I knew for certain what I had to do, and I knew I had to do it before I lost my mind or caught a case.

Paisley tried to talk to me a couple more times on the way home, but I wasn't trying to hear anything she was saying. My mind was running rampant all the way home. I just couldn't understand why I was hanging in there with her and all this bullshit. I did love her, but this was enough to make me lose my mind.

I pondered that thought as we made our way inside my condo. I had just removed my watch and placed it on my dresser when she came up behind me. "I'm sorry I told him about the prenup. I was just upset and needed someone to talk to."

I spun on her. "Upset? You know, Paisley, you're so damn stupid. All you had to do was say you'd sign the damn thing and I probably would've just torn it up. I just wanted to know that I could trust you."

She stepped back. "Oh, so this was a test?"

I looked at her and shook my head. "One that you failed miserably." I started taking off my clothes. I had just pulled my shirt over my head when a sparkle on her wrist caught my eye. "What's that?" I asked, peering at the expensive ruby tennis bracelet around her wrist.

Her eyes got big, and I could tell she was at a loss for words. "Wh-what does it look like?" she managed to say.

"It looks like a tennis bracelet that you can't afford." I took her arm and lifted it to inspect the bracelet. She tried to jerk her arm away, but I gripped it tighter. "That has to be, what, four, five carats? And it looks brand-new."

She managed to pull her arm free. "Well, it's not."

I glared at her. "Paisley, where'd you get that bracelet?" I know fine jewelry. That bracelet had to be at least twenty grand. No way in hell Paisley or anybody she knew could afford that. Nobody but Bobby.

"I been having it," she said unconvincingly.

"Paisley, don't lie to me," I said through gritted teeth.

She huffed and said, "Fine, Caleb. It was one of the gifts from

Bobby. And I'm *not* giving it back." She crossed her arms defiantly. "I gave back everything else you asked me to, but I spent too much time taking care of Bobby. I deserve something!"

I looked at her as if she were insane.

"You want to regulate how much money I get," Paisley snapped. "Then you want to turn around and have something to say when someone else gives me nice things. I'm sick of this. I gave back everything else because you're all insecure. But I'm not giving this back." She held up her wrist and shook it in my face. "With all this damn prenup talk, I don't know if we're even goin' to get married at all. So I'd be a fool to let you make me give everything back."

Now I knew she was insane. I swear, it took everything in my power not to go Ike Turner on her right there in my living room.

I stroked my chin, trying my damnedest to stay calm.

"You know what? Don't even sweat it. Keep the bracelet. Go get the car and all the other shit back—because I'm done." I walked over to the closet.

"What does that mean?"

I started pulling her clothes out of the closet. "I can show you better than I can tell you. Get your shit and get out. It's over. I'm done."

She looked at me in stunned disbelief. "I ain't goin' nowhere."

"Wanna bet?" I jerked a suitcase off the top shelf and flung it on the bed. "You can walk out with your stuff in hand, or you can get thrown out with your stuff right behind you." I stopped and stared at her. "The choice is yours."

"Where am I supposed to go?"

"Go to Bobby. I don't give a damn."

She stared back at me for a minute before finally stomping over to the bed. "You know what, Caleb? Fine. I don't need you or your cheap ass." She started stuffing her things into the suitcase.

I watched her for about fifteen minutes as she went back and forth from the dresser to the closet, stuffing everything in bags and suitcases.

Finally, after she gathered most of her things, she lugged them to the door. I probably should've helped her, but right about then I couldn't even stand the sight of her. I plopped down on the sofa and watched ESPN as she carried it all to the car, which she was lucky I was letting her keep.

After she finished packing the car, she stopped in front of the TV. I watched as she took my key off the ring and dropped it on the coffee table. "Here. I'm gone. Box up anything I left."

"See ya," I said nonchalantly.

"Fuck you, Caleb. Fuck you and your prenup." With that, she slammed the door on her way out.

28

Paisley

I felt like such a failure. I had hoped to go stay with Trina, but they still weren't through with her remodeling, so I was back home. Again.

I stood on the front porch of my mom's rickety wooden house asking myself if I would have been better off giving everything back to Bobby and just signing the prenup.

As if the Lord wanted to send me a sign, Mrs. Collings, our neighbor who had signed her husband's prenup, poked her head out her door.

"Hey, baby," she said, eyeing my luggage, which was sitting at my feet. "You moving back home?" She stepped out on her porch, leaning her nosy behind over the railing. "I would've never thought you to be one to ever move back here."

I contemplated saying something to her, asking her if she had any regrets about her prenup. But I knew if I opened my mouth I was going to cry, so I just waved and let myself in.

Walking in, I found my mother asleep on her tattered chair. She was leaning forward, her head bobbing. I felt tears pool in my eyes. She looked so much older than her fifty-seven years. Her skin sagged from her bones and her hair was severely gray at the roots, screaming for a color touch-up. A cigarette dangled from her right hand, and the TV was blasting *The Price Is Right.*

I eased the cigarette out of her hand and smashed it out in the ashtray next to her. Then I gently pushed her back and reclined her chair. I pulled her afghan up over her and leaned in to kiss her on the forehead.

Afterward I headed down the hallway toward my old room, taking in the numerous pictures my mother had hanging on the wall. I smiled at the one of my brother, Louis, proudly displaying his broken front tooth. He'd gotten that playing baseball and wore it like a badge of honor. I didn't even realize tears were trickling down my face until I heard my mother say, "Why you crying, baby girl?"

I jumped and turned toward her. "I thought you were asleep."

She smiled at me. "I was, until you broke into my house."

I returned her smile. "I have a key, remember? You can't break in with a key."

She didn't respond; instead, looking at the picture of Louis, her eyes began tearing up as well.

"I miss him something terrible."

I nodded, my words choking in my throat. My mother had struggled to raise me and Louis. Had worked around the clock. I used to think it should be a crime for someone to have to work so hard. For the longest time she refused to get on welfare. But finally she simply didn't have a choice. Her jobs cleaning office buildings at night and working fast food during the day just weren't enough to make ends meet. I think my mother lost her spirit the day she walked into that welfare office. She became a shell of her usual vibrant self. She always had been too proud to take help.

Not me. Especially after what happened to Louis.

My mother walked up and took my hand. "Baby girl, when you gon' let it go?"

I was hoping she wouldn't go there, but I should've known better. I opened my mouth to reply and let out a sob instead.

My mother took me in her arms and hugged me tightly. "Louis robbed that store on his own."

"Yeah, but—"

"No buts," she said, cutting me off. She looked up at the picture. "Your brother always was one to please."

"He robbed that convenience store to get money for me to have a stupid dress for the prom. My brother died because I wanted a dress." There. I'd said words I hadn't uttered in a long time.

"I done told you a hundred times, your brother died because he was doing something stupid, and you can't continue to beat yourself up about it."

"But if I hadn't shut myself up in my room crying my eyes out, he never would've tried to get the money."

"And he would've died some other way. It was just his time, baby. The Lord knows what he's doing. Paisley, baby, you trying so hard." She patted my cheek as she shook her head. "I'ma pray for you. I'm goin' to lie back down."

I stared at my mother walking away. She had spent many years trying to convince me that Louis's death was not my fault. She'd even broken down and sent me to therapy six months after it happened. But we didn't have the money to keep going.

Damn shame. Not only did I not have the money to get the dress, I didn't have the money to get the help I so desperately needed.

I think that's when I vowed to never want for anything again.

Maybe Louis's death should have taught me to be happy with the things I already had. But for me, it had the opposite effect. My brother had died trying to give me nice things because he felt I deserved them. I'd gotten sidetracked when I fell in love with Bobby and put up with his broke behind, but my vision was clear now. I deserved nice things. And the way I saw it, there was nothing wrong with wanting them. There was nothing wrong with not wanting to live in this dump like my mom. There was nothing wrong with wanting love *and* money.

My mother might have been too proud to ask for help, but I wasn't.

And as I looked down and watched a huge rat scurry across the hallway, I knew I couldn't be proud right now. I had been trying to get money on my own by being a model, or at least trying to anyway. But the model work wasn't coming and I dang sure wasn't going to live a rich life working these piss-ant jobs. No, it was time for me to forget love and focus on money.

I shivered at the bold rat that didn't seem the least bit fazed about a person being in the same room. I pulled out my cell phone and dialed Bobby's number. Trina's words flashed in my mind: *What one man won't do, another one will.*

29

Paisley

I released a long, hard yawn, followed by an intense stretch. I was surprised I made it through my daily workout routine without collapsing. That's just how tired I was.

I wanted to relax in the pool and have a snack on the patio, but who knew when Bobby would blow in? He said he didn't have a problem with me lounging around, but lately it seemed to be agitating him. It's not like I enjoyed it anyway. I didn't like being a twenty-six-year-old with no life.

I'd been at Bobby's place for three weeks. And honestly, it was nicer than anything I'd ever lived in before. We had fallen into a natural groove and Bobby was treating me like a queen, even balking when I suggested looking for a job so I could have something to do. But he'd started trippin' these past couple days.

The ringing telephone interrupted my thoughts. I walked near the doorway to answer the phone.

"Hello?"

"What's up?" Bobby said. I tensed up, not sure of what mood he'd be in.

"Nothing. Just chillin'." I even hated the sound of that. I made up my mind right then that if I couldn't find modeling, I was going to do something, even if it was part-time. I hated the way I was feeling.

"Would you like to go out for dinner tonight?"

"Sure, what'd you have in mind?" I smiled as I realized he was in a good mood. I listened as he told me about the restaurant at the new Hilton downtown.

"So you feel up to it?" he asked.

I looked at the clock and rolled my eyes. I wasn't planning on an evening out, but I could tell he really wanted to go, and that was enough for me.

After a long, hot shower, I started feeling better, more alive. I figured Bobby would provide an even bigger burst of energy when he arrived. He got in, showered, changed, and we headed out.

Every table in the Skyline Bar & Grill has a spectacular view of the city. The glass-walled restaurant is located on the twenty-fourth floor of the Hilton Americas hotel in downtown Houston. We were seated at a table along the glass wall, and I could literally look down at the ant-size people walking the streets.

I was looking forward to a nice evening. As the waiter approached, my eyes fixed on a man who walked in with a woman trailing close behind. Reginald Braxton. He was the man who had "discovered" me as a model and set me up with the calendar pictures that Caleb had seen on the Internet. Reginald also used to order my services for private parties. Tonight I said a silent prayer, hoping he'd act like he didn't recognize me.

There was no hiding in this place.

The instant our waiter walked away, Reginald seemed to appear out of nowhere.

Bobby and I both looked up simultaneously. A frown immediately invaded Bobby's face.

"Paisley? That you?" Reginald asked.

"How are you?" I replied, my voice bringing on a barrage of memories, most of them unpleasant. He looked over at Bobby as if he wanted an introduction. I smiled, trying to send him a mental message to beat it. To my dismay, he smiled back, extended his hand, and said, "I'm Reginald Braxton, an old friend of Paisley's."

I closed my eyes and sighed. Where was the waiter when he was really needed?

When Bobby looked at Reginald's hand, then looked up at him without taking it, I noticed his jaw tighten. I was preparing myself for the forthcoming drama.

"Well, she doesn't need your *friendship* anymore," Bobby snarled through gritted teeth. The smile faded from Reginald's face, and he dropped his arm and looked at me with confusion written across his face.

"I was just coming over to say hello; didn't mean to stir anything up," he said, eyeing Bobby.

"Now that you have, why don't you get lost?" Bobby snapped.

I didn't know if I should say something or just let the situation play itself out. Luckily, Reginald shrugged, then just walked away.

Before Reginald was out of earshot, Bobby turned his venomous words to me. "Who the hell was that busta?"

"Please, Bobby, can we just enjoy our evening?" I said, speaking as softly and calmly as I could, hoping he'd follow suit.

"That's what I was trying to do, but it looks like you still popular," he huffed. I don't know why Bobby was trippin'. We'd actually met at one of those private parties.

"You still messing around with that life?" he continued. "'Cause if so, I—"

"Bobby, please," I cut him off. "I haven't seen him in I don't know how long. Can we just enjoy dinner, please?"

Bobby rolled his eyes but didn't say anything else. We ordered our food and ate it with very little conversation. I was pissed because it wasn't the way I'd envisioned my evening.

Bobby's brows scrunched up. I could tell he was still annoyed, despite the fact that Reginald never came back to our table. Throughout dinner, I caught Bobby glancing toward Reginald's table.

"Are you gonna be able to get over this?" I asked.

"Am I gon' have to endure this kind of embarrassment every time I take you out?"

Without a word, I placed my elbow on top of the table with a thump and rubbed my temple. This nonsense was starting to wear me out, and I wanted him to know it.

The other day he'd come home and caused an uproar, demanding to know where I'd been during the hours of ten to two. He claimed he called the house several times and I didn't answer. I swore to him I never heard the phone.

The horrible argument finally ended because he had to go meet a client.

"Look, can we just leave? I don't want to do this here and now," I finally said.

"Fine," he snapped.

What had started out as a romantic evening quickly went south and resulted in us driving home silently and only speaking when absolutely necessary.

Later, back at the apartment, I felt a little awkward. He was still walking around with an attitude. I didn't necessarily want to go to bed angry but didn't feel like I should apologize for my past.

Bobby began undressing as he glared at me. "I don't trust you, Paisley. We might need to rethink what we're doing." He fluffed the top sheet on the bed, then flopped onto it, turning his back to me. He said it just as calmly as if he was telling me about the weather outside. That's when my heart dropped to the pit of my stomach.

I couldn't believe I was lying in bed with a man and we weren't speaking to each other. I was tired of this happening. One minute it was over between Bobby and me, the next, he's doing everything he can to win me back, only to get me and treat me like crap.

I felt like a fool for even putting myself in this position. I felt even worse when I closed my eyes and images of Caleb flashed through my mind. This had to be some kind of sick joke. I felt like a tennis ball being bounced from one man to the other and back again.

"This has got to stop," I mumbled as I yanked the cover up to my chin, squeezed my eyes shut, and begged sleep to take me away.

30

Caleb

"You look like crap." Dedra stood at my office door, her nose turned up.

"Dedra, I'm not in the mood, okay?" I replied. My life had spiraled out of control in the past three weeks, and I didn't know how to get it back. Hell, I didn't know if I *wanted* to get it back.

This was actually my second day back at work since Paisley and I broke up. I just couldn't pull it together. I almost called her many times and, in fact, had gone to her mother's house to ask her to come back when I noticed her leaving. Not only was she back in that Bentley, but I followed her back to Bobby's apartment. Bobby met her at the door and pulled her inside, his arm wrapped around her waist.

It hurt like hell to see that.

I didn't know losing Paisley would hurt so much, but I couldn't function for a few days after it set in that we were really over. I had to finally come to work because I knew Mr. Smith would be blowing a gasket about that Stackhouse account. Mr. Smith had called me a thousand times, but I refused to take his calls. I just couldn't deal with him. I'd had Dedra tell him I was sick while I tried to get myself together.

Dedra walked into my office and sat down in front of my desk. "Where is that kick ass and take names man I work for? I'm really worried about you, Caleb."

I smiled at her. She'd come over several times to check on me, and I knew I'd been a jerk to her. At some point, I knew I needed to apologize.

"Don't worry about me. I'm a'ight. I just need to get the figures together on this Stackhouse account." I started sifting through papers on my desk. "Where are the folders?"

Her eyes grew a sad look. "Mr. Smith gave the account to James."

My head shot up. "What? That's *my* account. I busted my butt to get that account."

"And James busted his butt to keep it." Startled, I looked up on hearing the deep baritone voice that was laced with anger.

Dedra immediately stood up. "Good morning, Mr. Smith."

He grunted at her, then said, "Will you excuse us, please?"

Dedra nodded, then scurried out of the room.

"You back from your sabbatical?" Mr. Smith barked after she was gone.

"Mr. Smith, I know I put you all in a bind, but—"

"*Bind* is an understatement! We were two seconds from losing a million-dollar account because you couldn't get your head together over a damn woman!"

My eyes grew wide. "Wh-where'd you get that from?"

"I run a multimillion-dollar company. It's my job to know these things about my partners, junior or otherwise."

"Well, Mr. Smith, it's not that. I was just . . . just sick."

"*Love*sick."

Mr. Smith sat down, and his tone softened. "Boy, I've been young and in love, but you have to remember not to let pleasure affect business."

"Yes sir."

"That's a cardinal rule, son." He paused. "And one you'll be well served to remember in your next job."

"Excuse me?" I knew he hadn't just said what I thought he'd said.

"Caleb, at one time you had a bright future ahead of you. I don't know what happened, but you got beside yourself. We lost the Hunt account and we almost lost another valuable client because of your ineptitude."

"Mr. Smith, please. I know things—"

He held up his hand as he stood back up. "No groveling. The decision has been made. It's not just that. Ever since you made junior partner, your work has been shoddy. You know your promotion was with a three-month probation. Well, we're exercising the option to release you within that period."

I was stunned. I'd never paid attention to that clause in my contract, because getting fired was never even on my radar.

"Of course, you'll get your severance package, but this is effective immediately. Now, because I like you, I've arranged for security to meet you back here tonight to clear out your desk so that you can leave with some dignity."

He smiled like he was doing me a favor. "Best of luck to you, Caleb."

He still wore that smug grin as he walked out of my office. I slumped to the floor in disbelief.

31

Caleb

"This is getting ridiculous." Dedra stood over my table with her hands on her hips.

"Dedra, leave me alone." I turned up my fifth glass of bourbon.

"No, I will *not* leave you alone," she said, sitting down across from me.

"You don't work for me anymore, so you don't have to care about me anymore. Shoot, you need to be worried yourself. You know if they got rid of me, they'll get rid of you too."

"And? That job is not my life. If they do, I'll figure something out. We'll figure something out."

I looked at her. Always in my corner. "Dedra, I'm no good. I can't keep a job. Can't keep a woman. Just leave me alone," I slurred.

"Save that whining for someone else," she replied.

I cocked my head at her. "I am not whining. I lost my job and my woman, Dedra. How am I supposed to feel?"

"You will get another job, and you needed to lose your woman."

Dedra took a deep breath. "She was never any good for you in the first place." Dedra said that like she was waiting to get it off her chest.

I felt my head start spinning. "No, I messed that up. If I just hadn't brought up that prenup. Or if I'd just been able to buy her more than he could."

"Caleb, love shouldn't go to the highest bidder. I think that was part of your problem in the first place. You know I never did particularly care for Paisley, but I think she genuinely cared for you."

I thought about it. "Naw, Todd was right. Paisley was a gold digger," I said as I sipped the last of my drink and signaled for the waitress to bring another one.

"But you turned her into one."

I stared at her. "What is that supposed to mean?"

This time, Dedra let out an exasperated sigh. "Caleb, have you ever thought about why you keep attracting these so-called gold diggers?"

"Yeah, they want my damn money."

"But how do they know about all your money?"

"What?" She wasn't making any sense.

"They know because you're always bragging about it. You flaunt it," she continued, pointing to my Rolex.

I pulled my arm back. "Oh, so now I'm supposed to walk around dressed like a bum so people won't know I have money? I worked too hard for everything I have."

"And I understand and respect that. But you don't have to broadcast it to the world. And you sure don't have to throw it out to the women you encounter. If you dangle a steak in front of a dog, naturally it's going to want it. And if you keep feeding it steaks, that's what it will become accustomed to."

I knew Dedra was right. I'd been thinking that same thing myself lately as I tried to figure out where I kept going wrong.

"I know you don't want to hear this, but I agree with Damon." Dedra's tone was soft.

"Oh, so now you're talking to my brother about me?"

"I'm worried about you, and so is he. We both think you're trying so hard to keep women from leaving you like your mother did."

"Dedra, don't go there."

"No, Caleb, somebody needs to go there. You got some issues. Your mother's abandonment messed you up, and until you deal with that, you're just going to keep repeating disastrous relationships like the one with Paisley."

I felt my head throbbing now in addition to the spinning. I didn't know if it was all the drinks or all the nonsense Dedra was talking. "Take that psychobabble somewhere else. I may be jacked up 'cause I keep attracting these gold-digging women, but it ain't got nothing to do with my mother."

"It has *everything* to do with your mother. We don't realize how a dysfunctional childhood can mess us up as adults."

"Who the hell are you? Dr. Phil?"

"Caleb, you can crack jokes all you want, but you know I'm going to keep it real with you. It's time to realize you're enough just as you are."

I stared at Dedra and for the first time saw how beautiful her eyes were. They were a light brown, slightly almond-shaped. And right now, they looked filled with concern for me.

I wanted to keep protesting, but honestly my vision was starting to get blurry. At the same time, I started seeing things I didn't normally notice before, like Dedra's eyes and her new haircut.

"You know, you really are pretty. Did you cut your hair?"

She ran her fingers through the feather-flipped do. "Gee, thanks for noticing, Caleb. It's only been two months."

Suddenly I felt really bad. Dedra had been one to keep it real. She'd been there for me through thick and thin, and I never even noticed how pretty she was.

I reached out to touch her face. She moved out of the way. "Caleb, you're drunk." She stood up. "Come on, let me get you home. And don't think this conversation is done. In fact, it's long overdue."

I wanted to respond, but by now my head was spinning out of control. She managed to get me to her car. "We'll just come back for your truck tomorrow," she said as she eased me into the passenger seat.

I closed my eyes as my head fell back against the seat. Dedra reached over me to fasten my seat belt and her scent filled my nose. I opened my eyes just as she snapped my seat belt in. I don't know what came over me, but I grabbed her head and pulled her to me in a passionate kiss. Yes, I was drunk, but I wasn't completely out of it. And I knew at that moment that all I wanted was to feel her lips.

She seemed surprised for a minute, but her body quickly relaxed and she kissed me back as she fell onto my lap. After a few minutes of passionate kissing, I stroked her face and said, "Come home with me."

She looked at me and I swear I saw tears in her eyes. "You just don't know how long I've wanted you to say those words."

I smiled brightly as images of our bodies intertwining began dancing in my head.

Dedra pulled herself up, closed my door, and walked around to the driver's side. After she got in, she turned to me and squeezed my hand. "And if the day should ever come that you say those words to me when you're not drunk, then I might consider it."

Huh? "So you don't want to make love to me?"

She started the car. "I want a lot of things, Caleb. Things I've been unable to have. And yes, I want you. But not like this. Not now. Truthfully, I don't know if ever. You have a lot of healing to do before you can have a woman like me." She flashed a smile.

"Damn, it's like that, huh?" I muttered.

She shrugged. "You know me."

"Yeah, you keep it real." I closed my eyes and leaned back again, surprised because I was seeing Dedra in a whole new way.

32

Paisley

"Love should've brought you home last night." I hummed the tune along with Toni Braxton as it played for the twentieth time.

The sun was coming up, and Bobby hadn't come home. I was more hurt than anything else. I had given up a lot for him and he'd treated me like crap since I'd moved in with him. That just pissed me off because he was the one who wanted me to come here. Maybe if I had fought harder things could've worked between Caleb and me. But instead, I let Bobby convince me that he was who I needed. My next mistake was calling Trina to vent. I thought I was getting a shoulder to lean on, but I should've known better.

"So lemme get this straight; y'all go out to dinner at that bomb-ass restaurant inside the Hilton. One of your old sugar daddies pulls a hater move, and Bobby's been trippin' ever since?"

"Yeah, that about sums it up," I said, looking toward the door and silently praying for Bobby to walk through it. He'd left yesterday afternoon and I hadn't seen or heard from him since. "Truthfully, though, he was trippin' before then."

"And tell me again why we're not out on the prowl? I mean,

how do you get over a trippin' man? Huh? I'll tell you how *not* to do it. Sitting at home, waiting for his ass to show up certainly is *not* the way to do it!" she snapped.

"You don't understand," I said, sitting up in my bed. "I can't keep going back and forth. It's, like, one minute I'm with Caleb, the next, Bobby's pulling me back, and I just don't know whether I'm coming or going. I don't even need to be thinking about bringing another man into the picture."

"Well, I can help you figure it out, and you my girl and all, but I'm gonna have to start charging you for this advice, especially if you're not gonna use my wisdom wisely. You sitting over there, crying over a man who won't act right." She tsked.

"Trina, if I followed your script, I'd have a new man every time the current one acts up," I tossed in.

"Yeah, and what's wrong with that?"

"Listening to you, I'll be running through men like they're going out of style. I can't operate like that, and I don't see how you do it," I said.

"Real easily. I mean, if his bank account ain't speaking my language, it's time to go check out the next man's checkbook." She laughed.

"Have you no shame?" I asked.

"Shame? Shame on me if I was broke all the damn time. I don't know about you, but I don't like being broke. There ain't no excuse for good-looking women like us to ever have man problems or financial flow problems."

"Well, no, not if every time someone acts out, you're ready to trade him in for the next big baller," I said.

"You make it sound so cheap. I trade up, baby, upward. And if there's no increase in the earning potential, then I'd just as well stick with the fool I know," she defended.

"Okay, Trina, I'll let you get back to sleep." I just no longer felt like talking.

After she grumbled a little more, Trina let me go and I tried to go back to sleep myself. I finally dozed off and woke a while later when I heard fumbling at the front door. *It's about time,* I thought.

I threw the covers back and rushed out to the living room, but I stopped in my tracks when I heard a female's voice mutter a curse word. Then the lock started to rattle again.

"Who's there?" I called out as I reached over for the cordless phone in case I needed to dial 911.

"Ah, I'm looking for Bobby Trumane," the female voice answered back. Now my interest was piqued. Who would be at our front door this early in the morning, trying to unlock it?

I looked through the peephole and saw a woman standing there. She looked harmless in her sleeveless silk top and black wide-leg pants.

"Bobby's not here. Is there something I can help you with?" I said through the door. She might look harmless, but I still wasn't taking any chances.

"Yes, you can answer a few questions for me," she replied.

I contemplated telling her to come back when Bobby was home, but she had made me curious. "Okay."

"Would you mind opening the door? I'm not trying to hurt you. I just need some information," she added.

I hesitated, then cracked the door and looked at her.

"I'll even stay out here, if you'd feel more comfortable that way." She held her hands up in surrender.

Once I opened the door, she stepped back a few feet. Her eyes glanced over me from head to toe, then back again.

"That Negro is up to his old tricks," she mumbled, shaking her head.

"Excuse me?"

She flung her long, auburn-tinted hair out of her face. "I'm Alyson Trumane. Bobby's wife."

I looked at her as if she had three heads. "Come again?" I said.

"I'm Bobby's wife. I found a few bills with this address in his car, and I couldn't help but wonder why he'd be receiving bills for another home, so I jotted down the address and decided to investigate."

"You're Bobby's *wife*?" I absolutely had to have heard her wrong.

"And you are . . . ?" she asked, with her eyebrows hitched up, but still far nicer than I would have been if the tables were turned.

"I—I *thought* I was his girlfriend," I said. "We live here together."

She looked at me as though she didn't know if she should believe my words. But a resigned look slowly crossed her face, like she'd been down this road before.

"How long?" she mumbled.

"I had no idea he was married," I offered.

"How long?" she repeated.

"I've only been living here a couple weeks."

She stood staring at me with a faraway look in her eyes. "I can't believe this!" she suddenly hissed with anger. I stepped back a bit.

"You don't know what it's like—what I've been through with him, and he has the nerve to be keeping his mistress in a whole other apartment!"

Mistress? I was somebody's mistress?

She shook her head. "I just don't believe this!" she hissed again. By now she was pacing the hallway in front of the door.

"He's cheated before, but never has he gone to this length," she snarled.

"Wh-where do you live? Because he's always here. Well, except for last night and when he's traveling." Which, come to think of it, was quite often.

"I live in L.A., and I work in the entertainment industry, so I'm on the road a lot. Bobby and I have been commuting since we got married six months ago. Six months, and he's been cheating five and a half of them." She sighed. "I just got in town last night."

"How long have you two known each other?"

"Since college. We've dated off and on for the last two years." She looked at me, recognition setting in. "You're the girl that busted him on TV."

I nodded.

She let out a pained sigh. "I never saw it, but believe me, I've heard about it. He told me that was an old episode from five years ago. And to think I believed him."

I walked to the sofa and sat down. None of this was making sense to me. *A wife? So I'd been the other woman all along?* A part of me didn't want to believe what she was saying, didn't want to believe I'd been that gullible.

"Where is he?" I managed to ask.

"I left him at home, asleep."

Home? "Where's home?"

"We have a house in Sugar Land." She looked like she actually felt sorry for me. "But he told me he had an appointment at ten." She looked at her watch. "So he's probably on his way there. Why don't you call him?" she suggested, her voice taking on an angry tone. "See what the bastard has to say for himself."

I thought about it. I really didn't want to get caught up in any drama, but this all had to be a big misunderstanding. And the only way to find out for sure was to call Bobby. I picked up the phone and dialed, half expecting to get his voice mail since he hadn't answered my calls all day yesterday.

"Hey, what's up?"

I caught my breath. "Oh, so you're answering your phone now?"

"Yeah, sorry. I had to go out of town on some business."

"And you couldn't call?"

"I was still a little upset about our argument and just needed some time. But I'm straight now."

Alyson was standing next to me, whispering, "Tell him to come over."

I inhaled. "Why don't you come by?"

"What are you wearing?" he asked slyly. I felt sick to my stomach.

I tried not to let him hear the disdain in my voice. "I'm wearing the negligee you bought me."

Alyson rolled her eyes.

"I'm on my way." He laughed.

I pushed the off button and stared at Alyson, who was standing there with her arms crossed. "Now we wait," she said.

33

Paisley

We waited about ten minutes before Alyson picked up her cell phone. "I'm gonna see what lie he tells me."

The minute she dialed his cell number, my heart started beating like it was about to leap from my chest. A thin layer of perspiration blanketed my forehead. I swallowed hard as we listened to the rings on her speakerphone. I was almost hoping that this could all still be explained.

"He'd better answer," she hissed.

I wanted him to answer, but then again, I didn't. I felt like I needed time to absorb all of what was going on. The truth of the matter was, I was in a real tight mess. If what this woman was saying was true, what did that mean for me?

Alyson stood, tapping her foot.

I wanted to yell, "Hang up, you see he ain't answering," just to buy some time.

"Hey, baby," his deep voice finally filled the room. "Where are you? I rolled over this morning and your sweet body was gone. I was hoping to get some this morning 'cause you definitely whipped it on me last night."

I closed my eyes and shook my head. My heart felt like it had dropped into the pit of my stomach.

"Alyson? You there?" he asked.

"Yeah, I'm here," she confirmed.

"Where are you? You sound like you're on a speakerphone."

"I'm in my rental car," she lied. "I had to go run out and take care of some business."

"Yeah, me too. I have that meeting I told you about."

"Oh yeah, the one with your client. Are you on your way there now?"

"Yeah, I'm about five minutes away. I'll call you when I'm done. I love you."

She didn't reply; instead, she just looked at me.

I couldn't help the tears that had begun to form behind my eyelids.

"Bobby," Alyson continued, "got a quick question. I found some mail for someone named Paisley Terrell. Who is that?"

He paused. "I don't know, baby. I've never heard that name before."

Alyson cut her eyes at me and shook her head again. "Didn't you date somebody named Paisley when we broke up one time? Isn't she that girl from that TV show *Busted*?"

"Oh yeah," he said, all smooth. "I haven't talked to her in years."

I couldn't believe his lying ass.

"Oh, okay. Well, I'll see you later. 'Bye." Alyson snapped her phone shut. "That bastard is just no good," she said.

We waited in silence for a few more minutes until I heard the key in the door.

"I'm going to the kitchen," she said, jumping up.

I stood in the middle of the living room and waited for Bobby to come in. Honestly, I wanted him to come in and tell me that this woman was some psycho ex who had a hard time letting go.

"Hey, baby," he said, trying to hug me.

I kept my arms folded and pulled myself back.

"Oh, so I guess you still hot about me leaving without calling? I told you, I just had to work out some things in my head. And my business trip was unexpected."

"Umphhh, I bet it was," I replied.

He tossed his keys on the end table and was just about to say something when his eyes made their way to the floor . . . and Alyson's pink Kate Spade bag. "Whose bag is that?" he asked, his eyes getting wide.

"Its' mine, you no-good dirty dog," Alyson said as she popped out of the kitchen.

Bobby was silent, I'm sure stunned.

"Oh, so you ain't got nothing to say now?" Alyson continued. She walked over and hauled off and slapped him so hard it dang near left a handprint on his light brown skin. "Oh, you have royally messed up this time, Bobby Dwight Trumane." Her calm demeanor was gone, and she was in straight "going-off" mode. "You've got a whole helluva lot of nerve! You swore last time was the last time and I was stupid enough to believe you. Oh, I'm taking you for every red dime you got, you'd better believe that!"

"Alyson! What are you doing here?" he demanded.

"You lying funky bastard! Is that all you can think of? *What am I doing here?*" She propped her hands on her hips and wiggled her head. "I could think of a few other questions to ask, and believe me, I don't plan to be the one answering them," she screamed.

I sat back, watching the exchange between my man and his wife and wondered how in the hell I could've read him so wrong. I gave up so much to be with him, and all this time he was married. My head started spinning. I wasn't sure, but I felt the veins at my temple begin to thump.

"And now *this*? Oh, you're outta your mind if you think this is just gonna pass," Alyson was threatening. "I'm calling my lawyer!"

I exhaled and proceeded to massage my temples.

"Oh, your ass is about to be wrung dry," she promised. "And trust me, when I'm done with you, you'll wish you never crossed me again, you can believe that!"

"Alyson, I need you to calm down," he said, stepping toward her.

She stepped back. "Calm down?"

"Yeah, that's right. I need you to calm down. Baby, I didn't mean to hurt you," he cooed. "Let's go home so we can talk about this."

I couldn't believe he wasn't even acknowledging me. "What about your girlfriend?" She pointed at me. I was standing off to the side, my arms crossed in front of my chest.

"I don't want her, baby. I want *you*." He never looked at me.

I wanted to curse him out, but I was scared if I opened my mouth again I would break down crying, and I wasn't about to give either of them the satisfaction.

I finally got the strength to speak. "Bobby, I can't believe you."

When he spoke, his voice bore a coldness I'd never experienced. "Paisley, I told you I was married, and that I loved Alyson," he said. He looked at his wife and added, "I started seeing her when we broke up, but I just didn't know how to end things with her."

"Try, 'I'm married,' motherfucker. That would have been a start," I snapped.

"You knew that."

I couldn't believe he was standing there, lying with a straight face. After I picked my mouth up off the floor, I looked at him, then at Alyson. The kinship she and I shared only moments earlier seemed immediately lost. Her eyes narrowed, and her hands went to her hips again.

She looked at me and said, "I thought you didn't know he was married?" as if that made his betrayal easier to understand. I wanted to know what had happened to the "funky bastard." She seemed to be falling for his pitiful apologetic act.

Bobby turned to her and said, "She pursued me relentlessly. You know I got that sex addiction, like Eric Benét. I told you I'm trying, baby, but she just played on my weaknesses. She was always in my face, throwing her body at me, telling me how much better she could make things if I'd only give us a chance. She even wanted me to leave you, but I just couldn't bring myself to do it, baby."

"I cannot believe this shit," I said, finally finding my voice. He needed to be with her dumb ass if she fell for that bull. "You can believe that if you want, but why would I be living up in his apartment?" I waved my arms around. "He moved me up in here. I don't know you, and I have no reason to lie to you. I had no idea he was married. You yourself said this isn't the first time he's done this. Hell, I busted him on national TV, so you know he's lying!"

When Alyson looked between me and her apologetic husband, I could tell none of that mattered. She was one of those "having a piece of man is better than having no man at all" women.

"I know your kind," Alyson said to me. "You see a man and his money and you think you've hit a gold mine."

I was stunned, truly undone! "I was with Bobby when he didn't have a dime," I protested.

"So why are you back with him?" She folded her arms across her chest and glared at me.

Bobby didn't give me time to respond. He stepped toward her again. "Baby, I just wanted some attention from you. Lately, you've been so wrapped up in everything other than me. Then the distance. I just wasn't sure you even wanted me anymore," he said apologetically. "I just needed to feel loved."

I leaned in and looked at him. Was that a tear going down this nigga's cheek?

I was thoroughly disgusted. If I hadn't seen this unfold with my own eyes, I would've never believed it.

"Bobby, you should know this is never the answer," she said, her tone softening. Next thing you know, the two were in each other's arms, and Bobby was letting out some fake-ass cry.

The sight of them both made me sick.

"Get the hell out," I said.

Alyson released herself from Bobby's embrace and looked up at me. "Oh, we're leaving all right. And you'll be leaving right behind us, because if this apartment is, indeed, in my husband's name, you have three days to vacate the premises."

With that, she grabbed Bobby's hand and headed out. Do you know that bastard left without even *looking* at me? I couldn't believe my life.

34

Caleb

I was actually excited about seeing Dedra. She'd called and asked if she could come by so we could talk. I knew I'd been drunk the other night, but I was definitely seeing things a whole lot clearer now. And I couldn't believe I'd been so blind for so long.

"Dang, man, why you standing over there, smiling like you won the lotto or something?"

I turned toward my brother. He swaggered into the room like he was Berry Gordy.

"Let's just say, now I see."

"Now you see *what*?" Damon plopped down on my sofa. "Never mind." He kicked his feet up on my coffee table. "Have I got some great news."

I swatted his feet down. "Let me guess, you got another hare-brained scheme."

Damon sat up, cheesing like crazy. "Nothing harebrained about this, man!"

"Would you spit it out? Dedra is on her way over here, and you need to be ghost when she gets here." I was surprised at how much better I was feeling. You'd think losing my job would've sent me even further into a plummet, but my severance package was enough that I would be okay for at least six months, so I actually felt more at peace than I had in a long time. Then there was this thing I was feeling for Dedra. Yeah, it was a little jacked up that I was drunk before I realized it, but I was completely sober now.

"I know you've been my financial partner in my quest to get Just Us Management Company off the ground," he said, referring to the business that he'd been trying to get going for months.

"I've been your financial *sponsor,* man. Partners contribute equally. You ain't contributed nothing." I laughed.

"I'm glad to see you're in a better mood, Bruce Bruce. But would you shut up and let me finish?" Damon stood up and walked to the center of the room. "As the creative genius behind Just Us, it is my pleasure to inform you, my partner, the financier of Just Us, that our latest artist, Sway, has just been offered a contract by Vibe Records. *Bam!*" He whipped a legal-size document out of his pocket.

I took the paper, my mouth hanging open. Damon started cabbage patching around the room. "Who's your daddy, who's your daddy?" he sang.

I looked over the paperwork and almost choked when I saw the dollar figure. "You've got to be kidding me!"

"No jokes, baby!"

"Can this Sway sing?"

"Obviously," Damon said, pointing to the contract. "You been so caught up in your own world that you haven't even paid him any attention. But he is off the chain!"

"Damn, man. Congratulations!" I was really happy for my brother. This was what he had been hoping for for so long.

"So snap out of this depression; we've got work to do."

I smiled. "I'm straight, man. I'm pulling it together."

Just then the doorbell rang. I answered it, and my heart warmed at the sight of Dedra standing there in a flowing prairie skirt and a sexy white tank top. Her hair was pulled back into a ponytail and she had on just enough makeup to enhance her beauty.

"Hey, you," she said, walking in. I wanted to take her in my arms and shower her with kisses.

"Hey, yourself," I replied, closing the door behind her.

"Hey, Damon. Why are you standing there all giddy?" She dropped her purse on my end table.

Damon walked over and planted a big kiss on her cheek. "'Cause we 'bout to blow up!" He headed toward the door. "Caleb, fill her in. I got to go find Sway and get his signature on this before something happens."

Damon didn't give either of us time to say good-bye, he was out the door so fast.

"What was that all about?" Dedra asked, sitting down on the sofa.

I sat down next to her. "Damon signed one of his artists—let me correct that, he signed his *only* artist—to a major record deal."

"Oh, Caleb!" She threw her arms around my neck. "I am so happy for you guys."

It felt so good to have her arms around my neck. I squeezed her. "Yeah, it looks like things may work out for me after all." I reluctantly pulled myself away from her. "I'm going to help with the financial side of things and maybe try to help get a few more artists."

That said, I gently placed my hand on her leg. She seemed a bit uneasy at first, but then she relaxed.

"See? You were all upset about losing your job. I told you God does everything for a reason," she said with a smile.

"You were right," I replied. We sat in awkward silence for a minute before it dawned on me that she'd said she needed to talk to me. But first, I needed to tell her what was on my mind.

"Dedra," I said, taking her hand, "you know you're my girl. Always have been."

"I know, Caleb," she softly replied.

"About the other night—"

She held her finger up to my lips. "Don't worry about it, Caleb. I know you were drunk and didn't mean any of that stuff."

I moved her finger. "Yes, I was drunk. But I meant every word. Dedra, I have been searching for the perfect woman, trying to find someone to fit in this particular mold. But the woman I was searching for was right under my nose the whole time. I was trying to find love, and love found me. And this time, I want to do things differently."

She looked at me with a confused look. "What are you saying, Caleb?"

"I'm saying I love you. I didn't know I did, but I do. You are my very best friend, and that's what I've been missing in all my relationships." I hoped she was feeling me. I didn't hesitate to pour my soul out to her because I just knew she felt the same way. I'd spent the past forty-eight hours tossing and turning, thinking about her. It was like the smoke had cleared and I could now see what I needed clear as day.

"Oh, Caleb." She buried her face in her hands. That definitely caught me by surprise.

"What? Am I reading you wrong? You don't feel the same way?"

She looked up at me. "Of course I do. I always have."

A smile crossed my face as I leaned in to kiss her. "Then what's the problem?"

She put her hand up to stop me. "The problem is, Marcus and I have set a wedding date."

I sat back. I definitely wasn't expecting that. "You're getting married?"

"You knew I was engaged."

"Yeah, but I—I never thought anything of it. You're not in love with him."

She shook her head. "That's not the point. The point is, I couldn't wait on you, as bad as I wanted to."

I lifted her chin and stared into her eyes. This was *not* happening. I'd finally realized the woman I needed to be with and she's about to marry someone else? I don't think so.

"Dedra, you and I were meant to be together. It took me the longest time to realize that. But now I truly believe the reasons my other relationships didn't work out was because God was saving me for you."

She laughed, definitely not what I was hoping for just after professing my love. "Caleb, baby, a month ago, it was you and Paisley who were meant to be together. I'm just a rebound. Your feelings for me are a rebound."

"No, you're not, and I resent that," I protested.

She stood up. "Caleb, that's what I came over here to tell you, that Marcus and I have set a wedding date. Yes, you hold my heart; you always will. But you have some issues and even if I weren't with Marcus, I just don't know that I could ever give you my heart until you deal with them. The prenup, the control, all of that"—she shook her head—"I couldn't deal with that."

"That's just it," I said excitedly. "I never even thought of a prenup with you. I would never ask you to sign one."

"You wouldn't need to worry about that with me because I couldn't care less about your money. I have my own. It may not be much, but it's enough to keep me happy." Dedra rubbed her legs. "But Caleb, that's beside the point. I just can't do this with you."

I was so not believing this. "So, just like that? You gon' go be with this man you don't even love?"

"Marcus brings stability, Caleb. You're a long way from that." She gently rubbed my cheek before she walked out.

I stood in the middle of my living room wondering how my joy had been deflated just like that.

35

Paisley

Thank God, I didn't have to go home. But I didn't know how long I'd be able to live off Trina. She'd already started acting funny and I hadn't even been at her place three days. What's up with people trippin' on me once I move in?

That's why I need to get my own place. I was kicking myself for giving up my apartment. Sure, I was getting evicted, but if I had really pushed it, the landlord would've let me stay.

I turned on the shower and let the steam fill the room. As I undressed I couldn't help but ask myself how many more times I was going to end up in this situation. I kept depending on a man. It was time I depended on myself.

I didn't realize I was crying until I stepped in the shower and felt the tears warming my cheeks. I just didn't understand why I kept making these dumb decisions when it came to men. Especially Caleb. Because through it all, I really loved him. I still loved him, prenup or not. I kept talking about him trusting me. Why couldn't I trust our love?

I sighed. There were no easy answers.

After I showered and changed into some lounging clothes, I made myself comfortable on Trina's couch. I had just started browsing the classifieds when she walked in.

I smiled and was just about to ask her about her day when she walked right past me and into her bedroom without speaking.

This was ridiculous. Trina was my girl and if she had a problem with me being here, she needed to let me know. Not that I wanted to hear it, because I definitely didn't want to go home to my mother's, but we still needed to talk about it.

I heard her bedroom door slam and decided enough was enough. I threw back the afghan blanket I had draped across my legs and made my way to her bedroom.

"Trina?" I said, lightly knocking on her door. "Hel-lo," I said, when she didn't respond. "So you just gon' ignore me now?"

When she still didn't reply, I felt myself getting an attitude. I thought we were better than that. "Look, Trina, if you have a problem with me staying at your place, it's no big deal. I can leave."

I stood for a few minutes, waiting on her to respond. I was just about to turn and leave when her bedroom door swung open. She was standing there with bloodshot eyes, her mascara running down her cheeks.

"Trina! What's wrong?" I asked as I stepped toward her.

"Nothing." She turned and walked back to her bed but left the door open, so I followed her in.

"Don't tell me nothing. You're crying. You don't cry." I looked on in amazement. Trina had to be one of the hardest females I'd ever met. She didn't cry over anything or anybody.

"Paisley, I don't want to talk about it." She plopped down on her bed. I was just about to say something else when she let out a huge sob. She buried her face in her hands as she cried and rocked back and forth.

Now I surely was scared. "Trina, sweetie, tell me what's going on," I said as I sat down next to her and gently rubbed her back.

"Paisley, my grandmother died today."

"Oh. I'm so sorry." I didn't know what to say. I knew she was close to her grandmother. That was really the only person she'd been close to in her whole family.

I reached over and pulled a couple of tissues out of a box and handed them to her. Trina wiped her eyes as she looked up at me.

"I know my grandmother lived a good life. So I'm sad about it, but I know she's in a better place." Trina toyed with a Kleenex. "But it still hurts. And it doesn't make things better that I called Roderick's house to tell him and just because I needed him to hold me, tell me everything was going to be all right, something."

"And?" I know Trina tried to act like Roderick was nothing more than a sugar daddy, but I think she really was starting to feel him.

"And he gave me his American Express and told me to go buy myself something to make me feel better, then he left to go play golf." Trina started softly crying again.

I was speechless.

"You know, the money is great," Trina said softly, "but I would've given anything for him to just act like he really cared about me. I'm so sick of these guys. Why can't they see I have feelings too?"

Trina was definitely ill, because I didn't think I'd ever heard her talk like that.

"I'm sorry Roderick wasn't there for you." I squeezed her hand. "But if you need anything, I'm here."

"I know you are," she replied. "I'm just being a wimp. I'm envisioning myself having to go through all of this by myself."

At that very moment, I think I realized how Trina and I had been going about finding love the wrong way.

I didn't mean to have any type of revelations in the midst of Trina's pain, but watching her there, so helpless, with no one to love her, well, it just made me know that I needed Caleb, for no other reason except that I loved him. And I needed to get him back, this time for good.

36

Caleb

It had been two days since Dedra dropped her bombshell and walked out of my life. I couldn't believe my luck. I'd been searching and searching for the woman of my dreams, and she'd been right under my nose the whole time. But now that I realized that, it seemed it was too late. I hadn't been able to get Dedra off my mind since she left my house two days ago. I wanted to call her, but at the same time I wanted to make sure I could do right by her.

I sighed heavily as I navigated my truck onto the Beltway. Damon and I had just gotten back from a flight to Los Angeles. We'd gone there this morning with Sway, signed a contract, and turned right around and come back.

Damon was sitting in the passenger seat, staring at the check in his hand.

"Man, you act like you've never seen that kind of money before," I laughed.

"I haven't. At least not my own."

"Don't forget, that ain't *all* yours."

He finally put the check in his wallet. "I know, man. Sway gets the bulk of it, then the rest, fifty-fifty."

"Long as you recognize." I honked at someone who was trying to get over. "And don't go spending all your money in one place."

Damon looked at me. "Man, I know you think I'm irresponsible, but this is my dream. I've been trying to get this management company off the ground for so long. This is just a start, and I'm not about to blow it."

I smiled at my brother. I was so proud of him and for some reason just knew he was going to be a success. That *we* were going to be a success. The record company was really excited about Sway and thought he would be the next Usher or something.

"So, are you rollin' with me to Mama's? You know I have to go by there and help her move that deep freezer," I said. My mother had been after me for weeks to come help her move the deep freezer outside for the Salvation Army to pick up. I don't know why Jenkins couldn't just help her move it. Regardless, I'd put it off for the longest, and since they were coming tomorrow, I had no choice but to do it today.

"Nah, man, I'm gon' let you handle that. I'm not in the mood to deal with Mom." He flashed a cheesy grin. "Just drop me off at my car. I'm trying to go to the bank."

I shook my head. "Whatever. I'll tell Mama you send your love."

After I dropped Damon off, it took me less than ten minutes to get to her house. She greeted me at the door.

"Hey, baby."

I leaned in and kissed her cheek. "What's up, Mama?" I said, stepping inside her town house. I was really glad she'd let me move her out of the small one-story we'd grown up in and into this spacious place.

We made small talk before I said, "Well, let me get that deep freezer moved." I normally would've stayed a little while and talked to her, but I'd spent the whole flight thinking about Dedra, and I'd made up my mind that I was going to at least try to talk to her about giving us a shot.

"Baby, have a seat first." She motioned toward the wingback chair across from her.

"Mama, I really gotta get going," I protested.

"I'm sorry. Did that sound like a request?" she sternly said.

I smiled and obeyed.

"So what happened with you and Paisley?"

I knew this was coming sooner or later. All I'd told her was we'd broken up.

"Damon told me she was just using you for your money."

I made a mental note to curse Damon out. "She was not using me for my money." At least I didn't think so. "It just didn't work."

"Umph." Mama tsked. "I've tried to stay out of your business and your pockets because of her."

"And I appreciate that, Mama. But I'm okay. Paisley is with someone else, and I'm trying to be."

She looked at me, concern etched across her face. "Don't you think you need to take it slow? You rushed into things with Paisley and look what happened. Take your time, get to know this new girl."

"That's just it. I know her already. I've *been* knowing her." I smiled as images of Dedra crossed my mind. "And she's feeling me. She's trying to deny it, but I know she's feeling me."

"You must be talking about Dedra."

I looked at Mom, surprised. She had met Dedra several times over the years and actually thought very highly of her. "How did you know that?"

"Boy, everybody knew that but you." She chuckled. "It was written all over that chile's face. I called her on it one time about a year ago."

"You did *what*?"

"I sure did. I saw how she was looking at you that time you brought her to your uncle's barbecue. And that wasn't nothing but love in her eyes."

"Get outta here."

"And go where?"

I laughed. "It's a figure of speech, Mama."

She shook her head like I wasn't making sense. "All I'm saying is that girl's been in love with you for a long time."

"She's never acted like it."

"Or maybe you were just too blind to see it. Plus, she told me she wasn't your type." My mother turned up her lips.

Suddenly I felt really bad. "She's just my type," I said. "But she's about to marry someone else and I think she's doing it for the sake of being married and not because she really loves him."

"Well, stop her," my mother said matter-of-factly, "because her heart is definitely with you."

I sighed. "She says I have some issues I have to work on." I looked up at my mom, debating whether I should continue. But something told me this conversation was long overdue.

"You do." She leaned back and let out a deep breath. "I know I'm at the core of those issues. Baby, I need you to let go of your resentment about me leaving. It wasn't about you or Damon. It was about me. I had you at fifteen. I spent my life struggling and giving everything I had to my children. It was wrong. But when I left, I needed to take my life back."

I really didn't want to have this conversation, but since she went there: "We didn't ask to be born."

"I know you didn't. And you were the best thing that ever happened to me. I'm not trying to justify it, but I just wanted a little slice of happiness. I just wanted to find me."

"But you almost lost us in the process."

When I looked at my mother, she had tears in her eyes. "Caleb, I am so sorry. If I could turn back the hands of time, I would do so many things differently. And I would never have saddled you with the responsibility of caring for your brother for any amount of time." She dabbed her eyes. "It hurts me to see you try so hard with these women because I know you're just trying to do whatever you can to hang on to them so they don't leave you. You think if you give them all of these material things, they'll never leave."

"If you had nice things, if you had money, you wouldn't have left. You would've been happy," I said. There was a hardness about my voice. I couldn't help it. I'd been wanting to say these things to my mom for a long time.

"Maybe. Maybe not. But the bottom line is, material things are *not* the answer," she said softly. "Baby, stop trying to buy love. You can see it doesn't work."

I took in what she was saying. What *everyone* had been saying. Was I that messed up over my mother leaving? Did I spend my money so freely with women because I thought if I did, they'd never leave? My mom was definitely right about one thing—it wasn't working.

Her voice interrupted my thoughts. "Find someone who loves you for you and the money won't matter."

I nodded my head. I'd found that in Dedra. I didn't know how I was going to change my ways, but I knew that I had to. I also knew, now more than ever, that I needed to change if I ever hoped to win Dedra's heart.

37

Caleb

I stood at Dedra's door, a confident man as I rang the doorbell again and waited. I probably should've called but I didn't want to give her time to think of all the reasons why I shouldn't come over.

I had just leaned in and tried to glance through the window by her door when I heard Dedra say, "Caleb? What are you doing?"

I jumped, then turned around. Dedra was walking up the steps, looking sexy in a pair of blue jeans and an I AM Fashions T-shirt. Why had I never noticed before how sexy she was?

"Yeah, man, what are you doing?"

I don't know why I hadn't seen Marcus standing behind her.

"Oh, hey. Ummm, I, ummm, I just came by because I needed to talk to you for a minute." Suddenly, coming over here seemed like a bad idea.

Marcus stepped toward Dedra, placing his arm around her waist. "What you need to talk to her about? She doesn't work for you anymore."

Dedra looked uncomfortable as she gently tried to squirm away.

"Ummm, it's some questions I n-needed to ask," I stammered.

Marcus nodded his head. "Okay. Ask."

I looked back and forth between the two of them. "Umm, Dedra, can I talk to you inside a minute?" I asked.

"Yeah, you can talk to *us* inside." It was obvious Marcus was not happy about me being here.

Dedra turned to Marcus. "Baby, thanks for dinner. Let me, um, let me go inside and talk to Caleb. I'll just call you later."

Marcus looked like he was about to go off. "And I'm supposed to just disappear?"

Dedra looked like she was pleading with her eyes. "Please don't be like that." She reached for him, but he jerked away.

"Naw, I see how you look at him, salivating all over him, like he would ever want *you*. You been pinin' after this nigga long as I known you, totally disrespecting me, and I'm sick of it. And you want me to be okay with him all up in your place?" He looked back and forth between me and Dedra. We both were standing there with looks of disbelief on our faces.

"Man, you trippin'," I said, stepping toward him.

He bucked up to me. "Don't tell me what I'm doin'. You got me messed up. You don't know me like that."

I looked at Dedra as if to say, *Is he for real?*

Dedra had a look in her eyes I had never seen before. "Caleb, maybe now isn't such a good time."

Oh hell, no. She looked afraid. No way was I leaving her now.

"Yeah, Caleb. *Now* isn't a good time. *Never* is a good time."

I swear he was twitching, and I was growing more concerned by the minute.

"No, I really need to talk to you, Dedra," I firmly said.

Dedra let out a long sigh. She leaned in and unlocked her door. "Go on inside. I'll be in in a minute."

I stood there. I was not going to leave her out here with this nutcase.

"Please, Caleb." She was now rubbing Marcus's arm as if she was trying to calm him down.

I could see the look of desperation on her face, so I went inside. But I stood right on the other side of the door.

"I can't believe you gon' disrespect me like that!" Marcus yelled.

"Would you calm down?" she said. "And keep your voice down. You know the neighbors called the police last time."

The police? What kind of mess was Dedra caught up in? I couldn't make out what she said to him next, but about five minutes later she stepped inside, by herself. She looked absolutely drained.

"You wanna tell me what that was about?" I asked as soon as she closed the door.

"*That* is my life." She walked in and threw her purse down on her sofa.

"That Negro is psycho," I said, following her.

"He's okay as long as he takes his medication, which I don't think he did today. He had a drink at dinner. I think that's what that was all about." She sighed as she turned to me. "Maybe we should do this another time."

"I ain't scared of Marcus's ass. Why are you? Do you think he's dangerous?"

"No, Marcus is a reformed choirboy. He just gets worked up sometimes."

"Dedra, what are you doing?"

Dedra had always been a strong black woman. No way would I have ever thought she'd put up with someone like that. "And you talking about marrying somebody like that?"

Suddenly her eyes filled with tears. "What was I supposed to do? Wait around on you to notice me, huh, Caleb? I'm not getting any younger. I want to get married. I want someone who loves me. And Marcus is a good man." She lowered her gaze. "Most of the time."

I didn't respond. Instead, I just stepped toward her and gently took her in my arms. At first she resisted, but then she let her body relax into my embrace.

She softly cried as I struggled to make sense of what was going on. This was definitely not what I had expected.

"Dedra, what is wrong?" I said as I eased her down on the love seat. I sat next to her. "Is he abusive?"

She shook her head as she wiped her tears. "No. At least not yet. But it's, like, the smallest thing sets him off and he becomes this person I don't know. The rest of the time, he's the perfect gentleman."

I leaned back, trying to process what she was saying. I was mad at myself that I had never taken the time to find out more about this dude. Dedra had always been there for me, and I had no idea what was going on in her life. I felt like crap.

"I'm sorry."

She sniffled. "What are you sorry for?"

"I'm sorry that I didn't know. That I haven't been as good a friend to you as you have been to me." I massaged the back of my neck. "Dedra, you deserve better than to live in fear of saying the wrong thing and making your man snap."

"It's not like this all of the time. Not even most of the time," she replied as she reached for a Kleenex on the end table.

I took this as my opportunity. I had come over here on a mission and now more than ever I knew I was going to see it through.

"Dedra, you are a good woman. A damn good woman. It took me a minute to figure that out."

She looked up and forced a smile. "A minute?"

"Okay, a few years. But I know it now." I took her hand. "Baby, I know you say you're about to marry Marcus. But I also know you don't love him like you love me. He knows it. And you know it too."

"How do you know how I feel about you?" she asked.

"I felt it when you kissed me. I can now see it when I look at you," I replied as I looked in her eyes.

She hesitated, then said, "But, Caleb, what about Paisley?"

"What about her? Paisley is my past. I want *you* to be my future."

Her shoulders slumped. "Caleb, don't play with my heart."

"I'm not playing, baby. I love you, Dedra, and I know I'm asking a lot by asking you to let Marcus go and give me a chance, but I promise—you won't regret it."

She sighed deeply as a pained expression crossed her face. I leaned in closer. "Just think about it," I whispered in her ear. Being this close to her felt so good. I knew I probably shouldn't, but I gently planted a wet kiss on her neck. When she let out a pleasurable moan, I kept going. I eased my way around to her lips, and we shared an electrifying kiss.

"Caleb, I love you so much," she moaned as I eased her up off the sofa and gently guided her to the bedroom.

Once we were in her room, I could see the uncertainty in her eyes. I wanted to assure her that this was for real. I lowered her onto the bed and stared into her eyes. "I love you too, Dedra." I was just about to begin kissing her neck when something stopped me. This was another part of my problem, I realized, bedding a woman too quickly.

"I'm sorry, Dedra," I said, pulling myself off of her.

"What's wrong?" she asked, sitting up.

"You're vulnerable. I don't want to take advantage of you. When we make love I want it to be special, not a rebound. And I want us to build our relationship before we go there."

A small smile crossed her lips. "I would've never thought you'd say something like that. But it means the world to me."

Watching her lying across the bed, I knew that my search was over. I'd found the love I'd been looking for.

38

Paisley

I pressed the end button on my phone after leaving my fourth message for Caleb, wondering why he couldn't at least show me the courtesy of a return call.

I had been down in the dumps for the past two weeks, since Bobby's wife waltzed into my life and turned it upside down.

I hadn't even heard from that bastard. God must've known I was at my wit's end because shortly after that whole episode I'd gotten a call from this modeling agency I had been trying to get with for three years. Now, not only did they want to offer me a contract, but they had some immediate catalog work they needed me to do. I just knew that was the start of something new, and that maybe I could finally get my life back on track.

Despite the fact that things were finally looking up, I found myself missing Caleb. Trina swore it was just because of what had happened with me and Bobby, but I really and truly missed him. And the more I thought about it, the more I found myself willing to put my pride aside to see if he would take me back. The modeling gig was paying well and it felt great having my own money.

But something was missing and I knew it was Caleb. I should have never left Caleb in the first place. I realized that now. And I figured whatever his issue was with me, we'd be able to work it out the moment he laid eyes on me.

That's why I'd decided to go by his place and leave him a letter. I looked down at the jasmine-scented envelope clutched tightly in my hand. I had poured my soul out to him. I hoped he was receptive.

I had just climbed out of my car when Caleb came jogging up to his condo. He was wearing his running gear, and his body was drenched in sweat.

I fought back a smile. Even better. I'd tell him everything that was in the letter in person. I dropped the letter in my purse as he approached me. "Caleb, how are you?" I said the moment he saw me.

"What can I do for you, Paisley?" he asked as he came to a stop. His voice was cold, not what I expected at all.

"Well, I was just in the neighborhood and wanted to drop by and see if I could talk to you."

"About what?"

"Excuse me?"

"You said you wanted to talk to me; what about?" he asked with no emotion.

"Well, Caleb, I was just thinking that we could discuss a few things, I mean, if you're not too busy and could spare a few minutes." I don't know why my stomach felt uneasy.

"I'm always busy, Paisley. We've kicked this management company off, and it's just taking off." He paused. "Besides, I don't know what we have to talk about."

I put on my pouty voice. "Caleb, why are you being so mean to me? I have some great news. I know we ended on a bad note, but we have too much history for things to be like this."

He laughed. "You are too funny." He looked over at my silver Bentley, which thankfully Bobby hadn't contacted me about taking back, especially since I'd sold my BMW. "But I guess it's all good. We both got what we wanted."

What was that supposed to mean?

I tried to tell myself that he was still mad because we had ended so badly.

"Can I come up and talk to you?"

"Nah, I don't think that would be a good idea."

I was just about to protest but stepped aside and let a couple pass on the sidewalk.

"Look, let me not beat around the bush." I stepped closer to him. "I made a huge mistake, Caleb, and I want the chance to make it right. I don't want your money. I just want you." I draped my arms around his neck. He took my hands and removed them from around his neck.

"Paisley, don't do that."

"Let me make it up to you. I'll sign your prenup. I'll do whatever you want. I just want us to get back together." I let my eyes roam his body. Even dripping with sweat, he looked so good. I wondered why I ever even considered leaving him in the first place.

"Paisley, I gotta go."

I grabbed his arm. "What's the hurry?" I asked, not liking the vibe I was getting from him.

He sighed. When he looked at me, I could see his anger dissolving. "Look, Paisley, I'm not trying to give you a hard time, but I just don't want to do this. I have a lot going on right now, and I don't want you to even remotely think we have a shot of working things out."

When I reached down and took his hands into mine and he

didn't pull away, I felt a sense of hope. I gazed into his eyes, willing him to want me the way he used to.

"So you don't love me anymore?" I softly asked.

"I don't know if I ever really did love you. Or if I loved the image of you."

That took me by surprise. I had no idea what that was supposed to mean. I was just about to ask him to elaborate when I noticed Dedra walk up behind him.

I looked her up and down. She was wearing one of Caleb's fraternity shirts and some Daisy Duke shorts.

I cocked my head and looked back at Caleb.

He smiled at her. "Baby, I'll be right up. I'm just trying to holla at Paisley real quick."

Baby? "Caleb, you want to tell me what is going on?"

"Ummm, no, really, I don't." He looked at Dedra, who had folded her arms and looked like she didn't plan on going anywhere.

"Are you fucking her now?" I was so not believing this. Had he been messing with her all this time?

"No, I'm not *fucking* her, Paisley."

I felt my heart relax for a minute.

"What we do is much deeper than that."

I now felt sick to my stomach. "So you're with her now?"

Caleb stepped toward her. "Yes, I am. And very happy."

I glared at Dedra. "You've wanted my man all along."

Dedra glared back, unfazed. "He would be *my* man now."

I was about to go off when I noticed a tall muscular man step around the corner.

"You scandalous bitch."

I recognize this guy, thought Paisley. It was Marcus—from the birthday dinner.

Dedra's confident expression suddenly disappeared. "Marcus, what are you doing here?"

He laughed as he slowly walked toward us. It was a deep, maniacal laugh. "You said you were breaking up with me because you needed your *space*," he hissed. "This don't look like much space to me."

"Dude, you need to jet," Caleb said.

He eyed Caleb. "*Dude*, ain't nobody talking to you," he spat angrily. "I *knew* you were after my woman."

I didn't know what the hell was going on, but it definitely didn't look pretty.

Caleb took another step toward Marcus. "Dedra, go in the house," he ordered. "Paisley, you need to get out of here."

Dedra eased back into the building, but Marcus reached under his shirt and quickly pulled out a small handgun. "Bitch, get your ass back here before I blow your boyfriend's head off."

Both Dedra and I screamed around the same time. The noise caught Marcus off guard, and Caleb used the distraction to pounce on him. Dedra and I continued to yell for help, stopping only when the sound of a single gunshot pierced the night.

39

Caleb

My head felt like a piñata at a five-year-old's birthday party. I groaned as I struggled to open my eyes.

"Where am I?" I asked no one in particular. The smell of medicine filled my nose.

"Caleb, baby, I'm right here."

I managed to open my eyes, but my vision was blurred. "Paisley?"

"Yes, baby." She took my hand.

"What happened?" I tried to move, but both my head and shoulder were killing me.

"You were shot. In the shoulder. Then hit your head on the concrete when you went down. But you're going to be fine." She rubbed my arm. I looked at her. Her eyes were puffy and her hair was frizzled. That was definitely unlike the Paisley I knew.

"Who shot me?"

"Dedra's boyfriend, Marcus," she angrily replied. "But he's in jail, baby. You don't have to worry about him ever again. I'll see to that."

My memory started coming back at the sound of Dedra's

name. I tried to sit up, but a pain shot through my right shoulder and sent me falling back on the pillow.

"Where's Dedra?"

"I'm here, Caleb," a voice whispered from the corner.

I turned my head toward the sound of her voice. She looked much worse than Paisley. Her hair was all over her head and her entire face looked swollen. Her eyes were beet red, and she clutched a wad of tissues in her hand.

"I'm sorry. I'm so sorry," Dedra kept mumbling.

"You should be," Paisley snapped. "He could've died because of you."

"Okay, girls, ya'll gon' need to take that fight outside." My mother walked over toward my bed.

"Mama?"

"I'm right here, baby." She took my other hand. "The doctors say you're gonna be just fine. That bullet hit you in the shoulder, but it went straight through."

"You are just lucky you weren't killed," Paisley snapped, shooting a scowl at Dedra. "All over *her*."

My mother gave Paisley a chastising look.

Paisley shrugged. "Miss Marva, I'm sorry, but if it weren't for her, we wouldn't be here. Caleb could've died because of her, because she was trying to play two men."

Dedra let out a small sob before turning and running out of the room.

I wanted more than anything to go after her, but it hurt like hell for me to move.

Paisley began adjusting my pillow. "Don't you worry, baby. I'm here, and I'm not going anywhere." She rubbed my forehead. I looked at her, suddenly remembering how much I loved her. But just as quickly, images of Dedra overcame those thoughts.

The night after I professed my love, Dedra broke it off with Marcus. She was afraid of how he'd react, so she did it over the phone. He had gone ballistic. She told him it just wasn't working and made sure that she didn't tell him about me. But she didn't have to. Apparently Marcus had started stalking her and had seen us together. He called, told her she'd be sorry, and slammed the phone down in her face. I had stayed with her all night, holding her and refusing to leave when she said maybe I shouldn't be around her until Marcus calmed down.

I had no idea things would end like this.

"I should've never left you, baby," Paisley said as she stroked my head. "Then you would've never tried to seek comfort in your secretary's arms."

I saw Mama turning her nose up. "I'm gonna go check on Dedra because I'm worried about that girl. She's been a basket case since this happened."

I could tell Paisley wanted to say something, but she let Mama go.

"Mama?" I stopped her right as she got to the door. She turned to me.

"Yeah, baby."

I removed my hand from Paisley's. I was feeling extremely tired, but I said, "Can you tell Dedra to come back in? I need her."

Paisley's eyebrows shot up. "Caleb?"

I raised my hand to shut her up.

Mama smiled and said, "I'll go get her."

As soon as Mama left, Paisley turned to me. "Caleb, I know Dedra might have been there for you for a minute, but she almost got you killed. I don't think it's a good idea that she be around."

I closed my eyes for a few seconds. When I opened them back up I said, "Paisley, it doesn't really matter to me what you think."

A surprised look crossed her face. "Babe, I know you're upset, but—"

"No buts, Paisley," I said. "It took me a minute to realize it, but breaking up with you was the best thing that ever happened to me." My voice was just above a whisper, but judging from the astonished look on her face, she heard me loud and clear.

Dedra eased my door open. "You asked for me?" she said softly.

I managed a smile. "Yeah, come on in. Paisley and I were just finishing up."

Dedra slowly walked in, uncertainty splashed across her face. I held my hand out to her. Much to Paisley's dismay, she took it.

I felt some of my strength returning. It was crazy, but I wanted to get better so Dedra and I could begin our life together. "Paisley, can you excuse us?" I said. "I want to be alone with my girlfriend."

"Caleb!"

"Paisley, sweetheart," Mama said, stepping toward her, "sometimes, all that glitters ain't gold. Maybe you'll get that one day. Maybe you won't." Mama looked proudly at me. "I think my baby finally got that. And I'm gon' have to ask you to respect that."

Paisley looked like she wanted to cry. It was a vulnerable side of her I'd never seen. "Miss Marva, Caleb and I were meant for each other."

"Baby, y'all were toxic. Like oil and water, cigarettes and gas, chicken and fish grease," my mother replied.

I couldn't help but smile because Mama was dead serious.

"And everybody got issues, but you need to find a partner in life to help you through your issues. That's what Caleb has with this girl." She pointed at Dedra.

"Mama, take it easy on her," I interjected. "It's not all her fault. I played a role in it by trying to buy her love."

"Don't get mad at me 'cause I speak the truth," she replied.

I looked over at Paisley, who was standing there clutching her purse strap. "Paisley, I'm going to tell you like a wise woman told me." I squeezed Dedra's hand. "You need to deal with your issues. Love and money are not synonymous. When things get tough, you can't go to the highest bidder. Yes, maybe I was wrong to ask you to sign a prenup. Hell, I have issues too. But two jacked-up people can't make it work."

Dedra, who was looking just as surprised as Paisley, said, "Caleb, I have issues too."

I turned my attention to her. "I know you're not perfect. But the key is, we're going in knowing we both have issues, and we'll help each other work through them."

"So you couldn't work through them with me?" Paisley said, her voice taking on a dejected tone I hadn't heard before.

"You never gave me a chance to see." I shifted, trying to get comfortable. "I wish you the best—with Bobby."

She cut me off. "I'm not with Bobby anymore."

"So that's why you came back," I responded matter-of-factly. The funny thing was, I didn't feel anger, jealousy, nothing.

Paisley looked at me. "No, it's not." She sighed. "I came back because I realized just how much I love you. I guess I realized it too late." She didn't bother to wipe away the single tear that had made its way out of her eye and was now traveling down her face. "Good bye, Caleb."

My heart actually hurt as I watched her walk away. Not because I didn't want her to go or anything. I just wanted her to find the happiness I finally had found.

My mother waited until Paisley had left the room, then turned to me and said, "I'm going to leave you two alone." She kissed me on the forehead before walking toward the door.

"Mama, did they bring the jeans I had on?"

"Yeah, they're hanging in the closet," she said.

"Where are you going?" Dedra asked.

"Nowhere. Mama, just hand me my jeans, please."

She reached in, pulled the pants out, and laid them across my bed. "I'm going to go call Damon and let him know how you're doing." She looked at Dedra. "Dedra, I'm happy you're with my son."

"Thank you, Miss Marva.

"Are you still with me?" Dedra asked after my mother left. "I mean, I won't blame you if you're not. I had no idea Marcus would ever do something like this."

I reached out and put my finger to her lips to silence her. "He didn't want to lose you. I can't blame him."

She closed her eyes and lovingly kissed my hand. "I was so scared that I was going to lose you."

I used my right hand to reach in my jeans pocket and pulled out a small box, the box I had planned to give Dedra the night I got shot. "Dedra?"

She opened her eyes and looked at me, the tears now flowing freely.

"You are everything I want in a woman and some of what I didn't know that I wanted. No one can tell us to take it slow because we've been friends for so long." I opened the box and pulled out the platinum solitaire. "I don't want to lose you either. Ever. So will you marry me?"

She stared at the ring. I'd gotten it the same day I was shot. It was about half the size of the one I'd gotten Paisley, but somehow I didn't think she would care.

Judging from the look of excitement on her face, she didn't.

"Are you sure?" she asked.

"Beyond sure."

She slowly extended her hand, which was shaking from anticipation. "Then, yes, I'll marry you."

She leaned in and planted a deep and ferocious kiss on me—one that warmed my soul. And despite the pain shooting through my right side, I had never been happier, because I'd finally found love, and the money didn't matter. . . .

READING GROUP GUIDE

Reading Group Guide

1. There's a saying that people are going to do only what you allow them to do. Do you believe that's why women continue to do Caleb wrong?

2. Caleb seems to have found the perfect woman in Asia. Do you believe he sabotages this relationship? Or do you believe they were never really compatible?

3. Do you believe it's Caleb's own fault that he attracts gold diggers?

4. Is it okay to take gifts from a man?

5. Paisley has gotten to the point that "it's just as easy to love a rich man as it is to love a broke man." What do you think of this attitude?

6. Paisley and Caleb seem to click instantly. Do you believe their attraction is genuine or are they both attracted because of what each brings to the table (Caleb, money; Paisley, appearance)?

7. Caleb's issues seem to stem in part from his relationship with his mother. How do you think his childhood shaped the man that he became?

8. Dedra obviously has feelings for Caleb throughout their relationship. Why do you think it takes her so long to act upon those feelings?

9. After the drama she endured with Bobby, particularly being humiliated on television, Paisley says she is completely through with him. Why is Bobby so easily able to woo Paisley back?

10. In Chapter 31, Dedra tells Caleb, "If you dangle a steak in front of a dog, naturally it's going to want it. And if you keep feeding it steaks, that's what it will become accustomed to." What do you think of this philosophy?

11. Caleb seems to be a mess when it comes to women. What do you think is the root of his problems?

12. After reading the entire book, who would you classify as the real gold digger, and why?

Please turn the page
for a sneak peek at

Je'Caryous Johnson's

next novel

Whatever She Wants

Chapter 1

The sound of glass shattering snapped Vivian Wolf out of her sleep. She sat straight up in her bed and immediately tried to focus in the pitch black.

For a minute, Vivian thought she was dreaming, but the sound of muffled voices quickly told her that she wasn't.

Vivian glanced over at the alarm clock. 3:00 a.m. The sound of more glass breaking brought Vivian out of her sleepy daze. She dove for the cordless phone, which sat next to her bed and quickly dialed 911.

"Hello," she whispered as soon as the operator answered, "I think there's someone breaking into my house." She pulled the covers back and eased out of bed.

"Okay, ma'am, are you in a safe location?"

Vivian quickly pulled the covers up to make the bed look like it hadn't been slept in. She then crawled under her king-size bed. "I'm safe for now," she quietly said. "But please send the police."

Vivian couldn't believe she was cowering underneath her bed. But since she hadn't listened to her boyfriend Marcus when he suggested she get a pistol, she knew she didn't have much choice.

Vivian's heart raced as she heard the burglars making their way up the stairs of her two-story townhome. "They're coming up my stairs," she whispered.

"Okay, ma'am, stay on the phone with us. The police are on their way. Can you get into a hiding place?"

"I'm already there."

"Okay, just stay there."

Vivian wanted to snap and ask the operator where else would she go, but she figured now wasn't the time to be going off on someone.

"I'm going to stay on the phone with you, but don't say anything," the operator said.

"Okay," Vivian said, her voice trembling. Vivian watched in horror as two men, dressed in black from head to toe, tiptoed into her bedroom.

The taller one immediately went to her dresser. Vivian grimaced as he picked up her Movado watch, her favorite gift from Marcus.

"Dang," the one at the dresser grumbled. "Ced, you did good with this one. We hit pay dirt!"

"Yeah," Ced, a stocky Spike Lee–looking guy, responded. "I told you. But man, I thought ol' girl was gonna be here. When I followed her home last week, I just imagined all of the things I was gonna do to her." He licked his lips.

Vivian fought back the terror that was building in her stomach.

"Where'd you find her?" the tall one asked as he started going through Vivian's dresser drawers.

Ced picked up one of her negligees, which was draped across her ottoman. "Spotted her at the ATM, looking all fly in her designer stuff and her convertible Benz." He put the negligee to his nose and inhaled. "She was yappin' away on her cell phone about how her boyfriend wanted her to move in with him but she wasn't havin' it," he continued. "I tried to holla at her and she blew me off. I was gonna teach her a lesson tonight. I spent all night dreaming about makin' her call me Daddy." He laughed and shook his head as if he was really disappointed that she wasn't there.

Vivian was glad she'd had enough sense to try and make the bed. She said a silent prayer that they didn't decide to look for her. She couldn't believe they had been planning to rape her.

"Is this her?" the first guy asked, picking up a picture of Vivian she'd taken at a Pinnacle Awards banquet where she'd been honored.

Ced nodded as he helped himself to Vivian's camera equipment.

"Damn, she's fine!" the guy said as he tossed the picture down.

"Ma'am, I know you can't say anything, but I wanted you to know we're still here," the dispatcher said through the phone.

Vivian wanted to ask how long before help arrived, but of course, she kept her mouth shut.

"Man, let's get outta here," Ced finally said. "For all we know she had a silent alarm or something."

They grabbed the bags they'd dumped her stuff in, then raced back down the stairs. Vivian waited for what seemed like forever, too scared to come out.

"Police!" she finally heard someone shout. "Is anyone up there?"

Vivian hung up the phone with the dispatcher, then slowly pulled herself out from under the bed. "I'm up here!" she yelled as she glanced over at the clock. It was 3:20. Vivian silently cursed. When she'd moved to this high-dollar neighborhood, she'd expected to never have a problem if she ever needed the police and now it had taken them twenty minutes to get here!

"Ma'am, are you okay?" one of the officers asked as she raced down the stairs.

"No, I am not," she snapped. "Two thugs just broke into my house, wiped me out, and could've freakin' killed me."

"Did they harm you?" the officer asked.

"No, because I was hiding under the bed like a two-year-old!" She took a deep breath to calm herself down as she looked around the living room to see what else they had taken.

"Ma'am, there is nothing wrong with hiding," the second officer, a woman, said.

Vivian held up her hands, trying to calm her nerves. "I'm sorry. I'm just a little shaken up."

"Do you have somewhere you can go? I'm sure you'd be a little more comfortable someplace else until we catch these guys," the female officer inquired.

Vivian glanced at the broken glass on her patio door, then turned toward the cordless phone sitting on her bar. "I need to call my boyfriend."

It was times like these that made Vivian wish she and Marcus lived together. Marcus was always trying to get her to move in with him. But he knew she was an independent woman and would never go for shackin' up. And since he'd made his feelings on marriage pretty clear—he was totally against it—living together simply wasn't an option. At least it didn't *used* to be an option. But now, as her mind replayed what could've possibly happened to her this evening, Vivian wanted the comfort of knowing her man was there to protect her. Her sister, Tracy, and her husband, Carlos, lived with her, but they were out of town. Vivian had appreciated having her house to herself once again, but now she definitely didn't want to be alone.

Vivian dialed Marcus's numbers and wanted to cry when he didn't answer either phone. Marcus was a sound sleeper and could sleep through a hurricane, so he probably was just knocked out.

After wrapping up things with the officers, Vivian eyed the broken glass and decided right then to leave. She raced back up to her room, threw on some clothes, and five minutes later was in her car on her way to Marcus's Sugar Land townhome.

Images of Marcus's muscular arms filled Vivian's head as she parked. Marcus was her everything. She'd had her share of bad relationships—men who just wanted to date the daughter of the wealthy real estate mogul Theodore Wolf, men who were enamored with her exotic looks and just wanted a beautiful woman on their arms. But Marcus was different. He saw her beauty on the inside. After her previous boyfriend had wiped out her bank account, Vivian had given up on love. But Marcus broke down that barrier and made her love again.

They had met at the gym. She wouldn't give him the time of day at first, but he slowly but surely wore her down. Marcus was from Chicago and had relocated to Houston to work in the business office of the Houston Rockets. He was everything Vivian ever wanted, and thought she needed.

Vivian thought back to the nightmare she'd just escaped. Those thugs could've raped and killed her. It made her realize that life was too short. She was going to tell Marcus that she would move in with him because she knew she'd never rest again in her home alone.

Vivian smiled for the first time that night as she rang his doorbell several times. She was exhausted and just wanted to get inside and fall asleep in her man's arms.

The door swung open. "May I help you?" the petite woman said groggily. It was obvious Vivian had awakened her out of a deep sleep.

Vivian leaned back and looked at the unit number. She'd been to Marcus's place only a few times, since he was always over at her house, but she could've sworn he lived in unit number three. "I'm sorry. I must have the wrong apartment."

"You must have," the woman replied.

Vivian was just about to turn and leave when she heard Marcus say, "Babe, what are you doing?"

Vivian's heart sank to the pit of her stomach. She looked over the woman's shoulder to see Marcus standing bare-chested in the Calvin Klein boxers she'd bought just last week.

Marcus's eyes widened in horror when he saw Vivian. She stood with her mouth open. The woman looked at Vivian, then at Marcus.

"What the hell is going on?" she said.

"Umm, nothing, baby. Gimme a minute," Marcus nervously said as he stepped toward the door.

"Oh no, I don't think so," she replied, wiggling her neck. "I'm not giving you anything. You want to explain to me why this woman is at our door at four o'clock in the morning?"

Our door, Vivian thought.

"Babe, just chill. Calm down," Marcus said.

"Yeah, Marcus, you want to explain to me why this woman is in your house at four o'clock in the morning," I said, trying to keep my voice from shaking.

"Because I'm his wife, tramp!" the woman snapped. "Where else would I be?"

Vivian stared at Marcus in disbelief. *"Wife?"*

"Did I stutter?" she yelled. "Marcus, you better get to explaining and you'd better get to explaining now!"

"Sweetheart, it's not even like that. Vivian is just a friend . . . " He plastered an innocent look across his face.

"Fr . . . fr . . ." Vivian struggled to get the words out but nothing would come.

"Friends don't show up at your house at four in the morning with overnight bags," his wife screamed, pointing at Vivian's bag.

"Marcus, would you please explain to me what is going on?" Vivian asked again.

Marcus looked flustered as he ran his hands over his bald head.

"Daddy, what's all this hollerin' and screamin'?"

They all turned toward the adorable little girl with long ponytails as she stood there in her Dora the Explorer gown, rubbing her eyes. "Why's Mommy yelling?"

Vivian looked from the little girl to Marcus. *"Daddy? Wife?"*

The woman seemed to calm down when her daughter walked

in. She glared at Marcus. "I'm putting Sasha back to bed. When I come back I want this tramp gone and you better get to talking." She cut her eyes at Vivian, grabbed her daughter's hand, then left the room.

The fact that Marcus kept trying to explain himself to this woman, and hadn't said two words to Vivian, made her sick to her stomach. Marcus looked like he had the fear of God in him as he watched his wife leave the room.

Vivian had to put her hands in her pockets to stop them from trembling.

"What are you doing here?" he finally said to her.

"Someone broke into my house and I just needed you. Please tell me this is all some cruel joke and you are not married, with a child."

Marcus buried his face in his hands. "Vivian, I am so sorry."

She let the overnight bag slip off her shoulder. "Sorry? Is that all you have to say?" She waited for him to respond and when he didn't, she asked, "How long have you been married?"

"Nine years."

Vivian was dumbfounded. She and Marcus spent a lot of time together, took frequent trips. How could he possibly be married? "I don't understand."

Marcus took a deep breath. "She doesn't live here. She lives in Chicago. We commute."

Vivian had to laugh to keep from crying. "This is freakin' unbelievable. You told me you loved me. You asked me to move in with you."

He just stared at her blankly.

"You asked me to move in with you," she repeated. "The whole, 'I want you with me 24-7, move in with me.' What was all of that?"

"Pillow talk."

Vivian took several deep breaths.

"I just got caught up," he added. "I never meant to hurt you."

Marcus's wife reappeared in the living room before Vivian could respond. A scowl covered her face as she folded her arms defiantly.

Vivian rocked back and forth. She was about to lose it. This could not possibly be happening to her. She had to get out of his apartment before the cops had to be called again.

"Sister, I'm sorry," she said, turning to his wife. "I had no idea."

Vivian shot Marcus a tearful yet hateful look as she turned and stormed off. Her grandmother used to always say if a snake bites you once, shame on it. If it bites you twice, shame on you.

Vivian couldn't believe she'd allowed herself to be bitten again.

About the Author

JE'CARYOUS JOHNSON is the founder, chairman, and CEO of I'm Ready Productions, one of the most successful theater companies in the nation. He is a national champion playwright and recipient of the NAACP 2007 Trailblazer Award as the youngest playwright/producer to create a formula for adapting best-selling romantic novels into national touring stage plays. He is responsible for changing the negative connotations associated with gospel plays into a thriving respected urban genre.

Johnson was the first person to adapt an African-American romance novel into a stage play. He was also the first person to write and produce a novel and a play simultaneously.

Today, Johnson is making his mark in film and television, becoming one of the most sought-after writers in the industry.

Johnson is also the author of the nonfiction book *I'm a Good Man . . . You're a Good Woman . . . So Why Can't We Find Each Other?* Up next is his second novel, *Whatever She Wants,* which is also based on one of his plays. He's also working on *Men, Money, & Gold Diggers* the movie.

Johnson's plays can be found on DVD at www.ImReady Productions.com and on his personal Web site at www.JeCaryous Johnson.com.